Sword Art: Online Alternative
Gun Gale Online
VII

4th Squad Jam: Start

Keiichi Sigsawa

ILLUSTRATION BY
Kouhaku Kuroboshi

SUPERVISED BY
Reki Kawahara

CONTENTS

DESIGN: BEE-PEE

Sword Art Online Alternative
GALE ONLINE VI
4th Squad Jam: Start

Sword Art Online Alternative
GUN GALE ONLINE
VII
4th Squad Jam: Start

Keiichi Sigsawa

ILLUSTRATION BY
Kouhaku Kuroboshi

SUPERVISED BY
Reki Kawahara

YEN
ON

NEW YORK

SWORD ART ONLINE Alternative Gun Gale Online, Vol. 7
KEIICHI SIGSAWA

Translation by Stephen Paul
Cover art by Kouhaku Kuroboshi

This book is a work of fiction. Names, characters, places, and incidents are the product of the author's imagination or are used fictitiously. Any resemblance to actual events, locales, or persons, living or dead, is coincidental.

SWORD ART ONLINE Alternative Gun Gale Online Vol. VII
©Keiichi Sigsawa / Reki Kawahara 2018
Edited by Dengeki Bunko
First published in Japan in 2018 by KADOKAWA CORPORATION, Tokyo.
English translation rights arranged with KADOKAWA CORPORATION, Tokyo, through TUTTLE-MORI AGENCY, INC., Tokyo.

English translation © 2020 by Yen Press, LLC

Yen On
150 West 30th Street, 19th Floor
New York, NY 10001

Visit us at yenpress.com
facebook.com/yenpress
twitter.com/yenpress
yenpress.tumblr.com
instagram.com/yenpress

First Yen On Edition: September 2020

Yen On is an imprint of Yen Press, LLC.
The Yen On name and logo are trademarks of Yen Press, LLC.

The publisher is not responsible for websites (or their content) that are not owned by the publisher.

Library of Congress Cataloging-in-Publication Data
Names: Sigsawa, Keiichi, 1972– author. | Kuroboshi, Kouhaku, illustrator. |
    Kawahara, Reki, supervisor. | Paul, Stephen (Translator), translator.
Title: 4th Squad Jam: Start / Keiichi Sigsawa ; illustration by Kouhaku Kuroboshi ;
    supervised by Reki Kawahara ; translation by Stephen Paul ; cover art by Kouhaku
    Kuroboshi.
Description: First Yen On edition. | New York : Yen On, 2018– |
    Series: Sword art online alternative gun gale online ; Volume 7
Identifiers: LCCN 2018009303 | ISBN 9781975327521 (v. 1 : pbk.) |
    ISBN 9781975353841 (v. 2 : pbk.) | ISBN 9781975353858 (v. 3 : pbk.) |
    ISBN 9781975353865 (v. 4 : pbk.) | ISBN 9781975353872 (v. 5 : pbk.) |
    ISBN 9781975353889 (v. 6 : pbk.) | ISBN 9781975315320 (v. 7 : pbk.)
Subjects: | CYAC: Fantasy games—Fiction. | Virtual reality—Fiction. |
    Role playing—Fiction. | BISAC: FICTION / Science Fiction / Adventure.
Classification: LCC PZ7.1.S537 Sq 2018 | DDC [Fic]—dc23
LC record available at https://lccn.loc.gov/2018009303

ISBNs: 978-1-9753-1532-0 (paperback)
        978-1-9753-1533-7 (ebook)

10 9 8 7 6 5 4 3 2 1

LSC-C

Printed in the United States of America

FIELD MAP

AREA 1 : Airport

AREA 2 : Town / Mall

AREA 3 : Swampland / River

AREA 4 : Forest

AREA 5 : Ruins

AREA 6 : Lake

AREA 7 : Craters

AREA 8 : Highway

Sword Art Online Alternative
GUN GALE ONLINE

Playback
of
SQUAD JAM

Summer 2025.

Karen Kohiruimaki, a six-foot-tall young woman with a complex about her height, found herself in the VRMMO of guns, bullets, and steel—known as *Gun Gale Online*—with a shrimpy virtual avatar well under five feet tall named Llenn.

February 2026.

At the invitation of Pitohui, a player she met in *GGO*, Llenn took part in a team battle-royale event called Squad Jam with a giant man named M against several six-member teams. She fought to the death against a group of powerful Amazons known as SHINC.

April 2026.

Karen was hesitant about participating in the second Squad Jam, but she changed her mind after Goushi (M's player) desperately pleaded with her to save Pitohui, because if Pitohui lost SJ2, she'd kill herself in real life

The only way to avoid this catastrophe was to complete a mission: Llenn's personal victory over Pitohui in Squad Jam. She enlisted a real-life friend named Miyu to convert from *ALfheim Online* and join the tournament—but the conclusion was unexpected.

July 2026.

After a three-month interval, the third Squad Jam sought participants. Llenn really wanted to fight this time, dreaming of a showdown with her rivals in SHINC. Her group, Team LPFM, was the favorite to win, but during the game, a horrible rule emerged: One designated member from each team became a betrayer, forming an entirely new team. Llenn ended up fighting Pitohui, whom she believed to be her team's betrayer…

And now, in August 2026, the fourth Squad Jam arrives. Llenn wants to fight SHINC once and for all, but will she actually get the chance?!

CHAPTER 1
The Things That Happened Before SJ4

SECT.1

CHAPTER 1
The Things That Happened Before SJ4

August 20th, 2026 (Thursday) Midday

"Why did I participate in Squad Jam? Because…a team-based battle royale sounded like fun? What other reason would there be?"

The answer was as breezy as the person responding was handsome.

"…"

Green-haired Shirley was at a loss for words.

She'd started playing *GGO* just to practice her marksmanship. She had no desire to shoot "people," but to be a team player, she'd accepted the invitation to join SJ2. Despite her reluctance, through some trick of fate, she'd discovered she was a devastating sniper.

Shirley turned to her "partner," Clarence, a woman good-looking enough to play a male role with the all-female Takarazuka Revue, and said as brusquely as she could, "No reason. None at all."

The two women were in hiding within *Gun Gale Online* (*GGO*).

It was a rarity in this game: a grassland zone. Despite the off-kilter red atmosphere, they were surrounded by knee-high blades of grass. It was a dull color, like green paint with a dollop of brown mixed in. It wasn't appetizing enough to try eating, no matter how starving you might be.

The grass grew thick and solid on the essentially flat ground, like a tasteless rug. The whole area around them had an eerie green color, and crumbled sections of concrete were scattered about, suggesting that people once lived here.

The two were lying low in this zone.

They stacked pieces of concrete around a slightly recessed dip in the ground, then dug a shallow hole and covered the edges with a large cloth that matched the color of the grass. They sprinkled ripped stalks on top for good measure. They had created an impromptu base.

The space was compact, just about six feet across, but it was enough for the two of them to hide facedown. It would be impossible to see their hiding spot for what it was unless one was both close and paying attention.

Shirley had her favorite gun, the Blaser R93 Tactical 2 bolt-action sniper rifle, propped up on a bipod in firing position. Its black muzzle hid in a small crack between two stones.

She wore her usual forestry jacket covered with images of trees. On her head was a baseball cap turned backward, with the same camo pattern printed on it, all but hiding the brilliant green color of her avatar's hair.

Clarence was lying prone immediately to her left—almost close enough to be spooning her—watching through binoculars. She had a handsome face, short black hair, and a generally low-pitched, masculine air. Most people in *GGO* probably wouldn't realize she was a woman unless they saw her character ID, which took the form of an in-world business card.

Like always, Clarence wore a black battle outfit like some kind of heavy special-ops uniform. Her magazine-pouch-lined combat vest was black, too.

Of course, she'd stick out in this environment in those clothes, so she was currently wrapped in a green poncho for camouflage.

Positioned before her eyes was a special AR-57 assault rifle. A Five-Seven pistol that used the same ammunition was in her right thigh holster. On her back, dangling like some fashion accessory, was a plasma grenade about the size of a mandarin orange.

*   *   *

They were both player killers.

In other words, they were *GGO* participants whose primarily purpose was to kill other players—PKers.

Rather than engaging in the typical gameplay loop of defeating monsters and killer robots or beating events to earn experience points, they aggressively hunted humans on the map for fun.

They didn't think this was a bad thing, either. In *GGO*, monsters weren't your only enemies. So here they were, in the middle of the wide-open field, hanging out in their own little sniper's den, waiting for prey.

"Hmm, no targets coming along," Clarence murmured—more like grumbled—as she stared through the binoculars.

Since they'd started trekking across the map, found a good spot, and set up their camp to wait, over two hours had ticked by. And time in the game world passed at the same rate as it did in the real world.

It was basically unthinkable to remain totally still in one spot for so long. Nearly every player would get bored long before this point. Clarence's and Shirley's patience and perseverance were remarkable.

Unfortunately, not a single person had passed by in that time—or perhaps *fortunately*, from the perspective of whoever might have gotten shot.

Shirley's sniper rifle was high-precision, equipped with exploding rounds that were essentially guaranteed fatal. Furthermore, as a hunter of Yezo sika deer in real life, she was an excellent marksman.

She could calculate the natural drop of a bullet over any distance all on her own, so she didn't need to make use of the "bullet circle," *GGO*'s offensive assistance system that showed the shooter roughly where the bullet would land.

That meant the defensive assistance system for other players, the "bullet line" that indicated its flight path, wouldn't show up, either.

The maximum distance Shirley could almost assuredly land a

shot was about half a mile. That was far enough that most people could barely see a person at all with the naked eye.

Any targets entering her "kill zone" would die one after the other by successive explosive rounds without ever realizing where the attack was coming from.

"You can bounce if you want," Shirley said bluntly, pulling her face away from her scope to rest her eyes. In this context, *bounce* meant log out of the game and go back to reality.

"It's no problem. I've got nothing to do today or tomorrow anyway. It's fun just being inside the world of *GGO*. Plus..." Clarence turned her handsome face toward Shirley.

"Plus what?"

"Who's going to watch your back if you don't have me?"

"...Good point," said Shirley, her face devoid of a smile.

In SJ2, Shirley had discovered that killing people with her sniper rifle was exhilarating, and since then, she'd obsessively studied the topics of sniping and snipers. She read books about the history of sharpshooting, watched movies about snipers, and searched for more information online.

What she'd learned was that, unlike what they showed in movies and comic books, snipers almost never acted alone in real life. A sniper had to have a partner, a "spotter" who carefully monitored their surroundings. That was true of police snipers going after deadly criminals and military snipers in war zones.

Spotters had a number of duties: keeping a wider eye out in all directions, measuring distance and wind strength to the target, communicating over wireless, and so on. They were also armed with an assault rifle to protect the sniper.

Shirley carried only a bolt-action sniper rifle, which required a manual pull to load each bullet, and a long knife called a ken-nata. She wouldn't stand a chance against a player bearing an automatic firearm or a group of monsters.

So having Clarence, with her AR-57, pistol, and grenade, was a big help when it came to protection. It left Shirley able to focus solely on her sniping.

Rustle, rustle.

Once a minute, Clarence would move, switching positions to watch the grassy plains to the right, left, or rear with her binoculars. It often meant that Clarence rested her stomach against Shirley's butt in an overlapping cross, but Shirley didn't complain, of course, and it caused no system warning against sexual harassment.

Clarence had finished checking their surroundings from under the tarp covering their little base, and there was nothing moving out there, whether player character or monster. There wasn't even any breeze over the grass.

"All green, then," she said, rotating herself carefully to face forward again. She peered through the binoculars, searching for potential targets. Without turning her head toward Shirley, she said, "By the way, about that…"

"About what?" asked Shirley, right eye to the rifle scope, left eye still open. In *GGO*, it wasn't rude at all to speak to someone without looking at them. Better to keep your eyes trained on the area around you.

Some people who got way into *GGO* found they developed a habit of keeping an eye trained for danger even in real life, to the point where it affected their regular lives.

Clarence explained, "The reason I play in Squad Jam. Well, I was in SJ2 with my squadron, but nobody else wanted to join when SJ3 rolled around."

"Mmm." Shirley wasn't that interested in her story. However, because there wasn't currently any prey to shoot, she had no choice but to listen.

That made her realize something. Without taking her eye away from the scope, she said, "Hang on. You *were* in SJ3, though."

"Yeah, I was. I mean, duh."

They met after engaging in a tremendous one-on-one battle to the death in SJ3, so of course they remembered it.

"I wasn't done with the story. I *asked* them to help us fight as a team of six in the preliminary round, but in the final event, it was just me and Sam."

"Ah, yeah, that's right."

What Shirley didn't know—and what Clarence was avoiding saying—was that she'd threatened her squadmates into participating. Clarence had entered the final as a pair with her teammate Sam, and it was Shirley who'd slaughtered him with an exploding round.

"I should have shot you first," Shirley said sadly, but she hadn't had a choice, given the circumstances.

Sam had been standing behind Clarence. When the person in front gets sniped, the person in back instinctively ducks down out of danger. When the person in the back gets shot, though, the one in front always turns around, making them an easy target. Shirley's strategy was solid.

Clarence did turn away, in fact, but Shirley's second shot was a bit delayed, giving her prey time for evasive maneuvers. Shirley replayed the sequence in her head and said ruefully, "It's the biggest regret of my *GGO* life."

"Well, that's not coming back around."

"Heh."

"Anyway, as for Sam, he really didn't seem to like my Super-Awesome Betrayal plan…," Clarence said, pouting.

They had participated in a plan among the lesser squads to fight together against one of the heavyweights, but then Clarence had betrayed them, shooting them in the back. Sam was merely an unhappy accomplice.

Of course, SJ3 itself later implemented a special rule that forced chosen players to form a team of betrayers. It was a deeply unpopular change among the tournament participants. It hadn't affected Clarence or Shirley, though, because they'd killed each other before it got to that point.

"Poor little me—removed from my squadron. Stripped of all rank and privilege. In fact, my only registered friend in the game now is the lovely Shirley."

"I don't blame them, knowing how crazy you are. They must be pretty nice if all they did was kick you out. Did you pay them back?"

"Wow, you are brutally frank, you know that? Don't you know what an embolism is?"

"Of course. It's a kind of blood clot."

"Huh...? No! Crap! I meant euphemism! Don't you know how to mince words, Shirley?"

"I don't want to hear that from *you*. But don't get the wrong idea—I'm not criticizing your insane actions."

"You aren't?"

"That's right. This is a game. My game self and my real self are different...and that stands to reason."

"Treason? Are you a traitor?" Clarence asked, all innocently. Shirley, annoyed, narrowed her eyes.

"Have you actually had your compulsory education?"

"Not to my knowledge."

"...Well, what I meant was, they're supposed to be different."

"That's exactly it!"

"What is?"

"The reason I teamed up with you, Shirley! In real life, I would never work with such a menacing and dangerous person!"

"Keh!" Shirley snapped, but now there was a grin on her lips. Not that Clarence could see it with her attention on the binoculars.

Shirley clutched her sniper rifle and muttered, "This is a game. Killing people with a rifle and stabbing them with a ken-nata are things you do *because* it's a game. I'd never do these things in real life. Not even if I was going to die. I wouldn't consider it for even a second."

In real life, Shirley was a twenty-four-year-old woman by the name of Mai Kirishima. She lived in Hokkaido, where she worked as a nature guide and hunter. She owned a hunting rifle for which she'd gotten a permit in accordance with Japanese law. Her claim had weight behind it.

It was the kind of statement that deserved to be heard by the big shots who claimed that "gamer brain" was a thing—that playing video games limited a person's ability to distinguish games from reality—even though they'd never had any experience playing games themselves.

Beneath the binoculars, Clarence's mouth curled into a grin. "Yeah, I'm a saint in real life, too. If memory serves, I've never once shot a person to death in the real world."

"Then I'll have to pray for the accuracy of your memory."

"I'm not old enough to be going senile."

They spoke very openly and bluntly, but whether in a full-dive VR setting or not, any online game where players used avatars as fictional personas wasn't somewhere you were supposed to ask others details about someone's real life.

If you wanted to reveal specifics about yourself, that was up to you, of course. It was also evidence that the two of them were reasonably friendly. It was common in online games to share more and more detail over time, until you knew so much about the other player that it seemed pointless not to meet up in person.

"So what I'm saying is…," Clarence prompted, pulling away from the binoculars.

"Hmm?"

Shirley glanced to her left, sensing Clarence's eyes on her. She saw a handsome face with a very expectant smile.

"Let's meet up in person! I'll visit you!"

"Ugh, not this again…"

Shirley frowned a bit. Since her partner was so insistent, though, she gave away a snippet of information. "I live on the outskirts of Japan. You still think you could make it?"

"Is it far? Far from Tokyo? Like, a pretty expensive bus trip?"

"So you live in Tokyo."

"H-how did you figure that out…? Wait, are you psychic?"

"Well, you're pretty far away from me. Buses in real life can't cross the ocean."

"What? You live in another country?" Clarence asked, shocked.

Shirley repeated her jab from earlier. "Have you actually completed your compulsory education?"

"Not to my knowledge."

"We're playing *GGO* on the Japan server, so of course I live in Japan. On the very edge of Japan. On a different island than Honshu."

"Ohhh, so you're far away. Yeah, that might be tough, then," said Clarence in what passed for a gloomy tone by her standards.

"…" Shirley was taken aback by her reaction. "All I'm saying is maybe it's not meant to happen. We can easily meet up here—it's fine," she said reassuringly.

"Mmm." Clarence pouted, returning to her binoculars. She had forgotten to execute her customary check of the surroundings, which she'd been doing every minute previously.

"By the way," said Shirley, changing the subject and not scolding her for being forgetful.

"Whut?"

"If there's another Squad Jam, are you in?"

"You bet I am!" Clarence exclaimed. "Let's go in together, like with that playtest! Just the two of us, on a huge map, against a ton of enemies! Yahoo!" Despite the cramped area, she kicked and fidgeted like a child.

"Don't lose control of yourself in here," Shirley snapped. "Anyway, I'm all right with that, but…"

She trailed off. Clarence stopped squirming, sensing the answer already. She made what qualified as a somber look by her standards. "Yeah, I get it. The prelims are always tough…"

"That's the problem."

The source of their gloom was Squad Jam's preliminary round. With the increase in teams wanting to enter, there was now a seeding system in which the top four teams from last event got a bye, while everyone else had to win a preliminary competition to place in the finals.

It was a head-to-head, two-team match taking place on a long, narrow map. Since Squad Jam featured six-person teams, trying to win the prelims with a two-person squad that specialized in sniping would be very difficult.

In SJ3, Shirley got through the preliminary round with Team

KKHC, the Kita no Kuni Hunter's Club. Clarence threatened her teammates to get a group of six just for the prelims.

They wouldn't be able to use that strategy this time.

The rest of KKHC had been inching away from *GGO*, intimidated by Shirley's intensity, and Clarence's teammates had plain ditched her.

"What should we do?"

"What should we do?"

They sighed in unison.

Then a voice from above said, "I've got a great idea!"

"Aaah!" "Aieee!"

The two women bounced straight upward from their prone positions, like a gag in a comic book. They turned to face the cloth draped over their hiding spot, but it had been torn away, revealing the red sky. Against the light, pointing the muzzle of an assault rifle in their direction, was a woman wearing a lumpy green suit.

"Dammit—!"

Shirley twisted, trying to point the R93 Tactical 2 at the enemy, despite knowing there was no way she'd make it in time.

Shpak!

A bullet went through her shoulder.

"Fiiinally found you! Man, it was hard to track you down!"

There stood Pitohui, canvas shelter sheet in one hand, HK416C shortened assault rifle that she'd used in the recent playtest in the other. It was aimed right between Shirley's furious eyes.

The lumpy, all-green outfit she wore made her resemble some forest fairy. That was thanks to the ghillie suit—a type of camouflage with strips and scraps of fine fabric that completely hid the user when worn against a background of the same color, as long as she didn't move.

Pitohui even wore camouflage face paint, covering up her famous cheek tattoos. Her gun was green as well.

"Goddamn you!" Shirley swore, her angriest outburst of the

day. Bright-red polygonal effects shone from her shoulder, the visual sign of damage unique to *GGO*'s bullet wounds. A bullet line pointed directly at the center of her chest.

"Oh my!" exclaimed Clarence, her eyes wide. Then she said, "Oh, Shirley? Just so I'm not confused, when you said 'Goddamn you,' you weren't referring to me, right? I mean, I know I kinda slacked off on keeping an eye out for a bit, but that was because I was so engaged in our conversation, and you totally forgot, too! And you didn't warn me to pay attention!"

"Shut up and shoot her! Do it right now!"

"No way! If I shoot now, she'll shoot and kill *you*."

"...Why are you bothered by that?!"

"I'm not! But I'm gonna get shot and killed after that, too! I don't want that!"

"*That's* your argument?!"

"Yes!"

At the end of this little comedy routine, Pitohui glanced at Clarence. She still had her finger on the trigger of the HK416C, of course.

"That's very perceptive of you, little Miss Takarazuka. This is our first real conversation, isn't it? *My name is Pitohui. Nice to meet you,*" she said, dipping into a different language at the end.

"Whoa. I got complimented? Nice to meet you, crazy ponytail face-tattoo lady who kicked all kinds of ass in SJ2 and SJ3. My name's Clarence. By the way, what language was that at the end?"

"It's called English. Ever heard of it?"

"Oh! English! Yeah, I know that one! It's the language my English teacher can't speak!"

"You're very funny, Clare," said Pitohui. The pair seemed made for each other.

"Enough of this, you two!" snapped Shirley. Despite the gun pointed at her chest, she mounted a verbal assault. "Pitohui! How dare you shoot me! I'll kill you someday! Remember that! Don't forget it!"

It was none other than Pitohui who'd helped turn Shirley into the person she was today.

A game was a game, so she didn't bear a true personal grudge, but if Shirley saw her rival on the battlefield, she would absolutely aim to shoot and destroy her. Consequently, completely losing the initiative and being conquered without a chance to fire was supremely frustrating. No wonder she was swearing.

Pitohui just grinned and said seriously, "Very scary. You got me with a good shot in SJ2, if I recall. I'd have died if it had been an exploding round—of course I'm going to be careful around you."

"Keh!"

"Anyway, I didn't come here to talk about this today. Can I move on to the point of this interaction?"

"Sure thing!" Clarence chirped.

"Wait! What do you mean, 'the point'? What you came to talk about? You weren't trying to kill us?" Shirley demanded, shocked.

GGO was a game that was very proactive and friendly in encouraging its players to kill one another. With her sudden appearance, Shirley had just assumed Pitohui was attacking them. Could she have been wrong?

"*Non, non, non!* I'm here to talk! Words! Dialogue! Get it?"

Shirley was stunned. Eventually, she exhaled, the tension easing from her shoulders. "Speak, then…"

"Okay! The thing is, I've been searching for you two ever since that playtest, but I couldn't find you in town at all. Eventually, my search took me out into the wilderness! And I finally found you about three hours ago! This is my lucky day!"

"What's that supposed to mean…?" grumbled Shirley. The anger was gone, replaced by exasperation. The expression on her face said she was in the presence of an unbelievable idiot. "So you've been waiting to sneak up on us since the moment we set up our sniping position?"

"That's right."

"How?" Shirley wondered, truly curious.

"Yeah! I was keeping a strict eye out! Until the last minute, that is!" Clarence added, outraged.

"I did it with an army crawl, of course. From about two-thirds of a mile away? Crawling the entire way. I knew that Clare was doing a full perimeter search over the course of each minute, though, so…"

Pitohui tapped her ear, a gesture that indicated she was using a communication item. Then she pointed to the sky.

"I had a friend in a much more distant location watching you like a hawk."

In other words, M was somewhere else, observing from far above with the drone he'd bought for the playtest and practiced with since. He'd been giving Pitohui directions based on what he saw.

Shirley and Clarence were stunned—

"What the hell…?"

"Whoa, that's amazing!"

—stunned or annoyed, or maybe a bit of both.

Even with the backup, she'd army-crawled the better part of a mile for two hours. Moving slowly, sometimes stopping, then resuming, all to ensure she wasn't spotted…

For both the person making the approach and the one providing direction, this was an even more superhuman feat of patience than Shirley and Clarence's use of their sniping hideout.

Real war was one thing, but this was a VR game. People didn't bother with these things.

"And then, once I got close enough that there was no way to hide if you looked at me, that's when it was really tough. I waited a really long time for my chance to arrive, and therefore, now I have appeared."

"Wow, that's amazing!"

Clap, clap, clap, clap, clap. Clarence forgot about her weapon and started a round of applause instead.

"…" Shirley shot her a withering glance but said nothing.

"Anyway, back to the point. I have gone to these great lengths to bring you two an invitation! To what? Do I really need to say it? You know what it is, right? I mean, it would be crazy if you didn't, right?"

"…" Shirley immediately knew what it was but didn't say a word.

"I got it!" said Clarence, a second later. "The next Squad Jam! Your team has that man as big as a mountain, and—"

"That's M."

"—the tiny little pink one, and—"

"That's Llenn."

"—the tiny little grenadier!"

"That's Fukaziroh."

"That's only four, and you want the two of us to fill it to maximum!"

"Correct! Brilliant!" Pitohui crowed, grinning. The combination of her green face and wicked smile was positively demonic.

Shirley asked the demon, "What...are you thinking...? You know that I'm just dying to kill you..."

"Yeah, you said that already. Why would that be a reason not to team up?"

"..."

Shirley had no quick answer to that.

"She's right, Shirley! We should join them already! That way we won't have to fight in the prelims! And when the final event starts, you can shoot her in the back!" Clarence suggested. Nobody could accuse her of not being true to herself.

Pitohui said, "Well, I'm fine with that. If you want, the two of you can even break off from us right at the start and do your own thing."

"Really? Yippee! We're in, we're in! Hey, you wanna friend me?"

"Sure thing! One friend, coming up!"

"..."

With undisguised annoyance, Shirley watched the two frolic. Eventually, though, she made up her mind. There wasn't a better way to get into Squad Jam at this point, she realized.

She looked past the muzzle of the gun Pitohui still had pointed at her and grunted, as though wringing her voice from the depths of hell. "Fine. I'll join your squad this time. And..."

"And?"

"I'll do whatever I want as soon as it starts. If I get the chance, I'm going to shoot you!"

"Can't wait! Let's go with that plan, then!" said Pitohui. She let the HK416C drift away.

Shirley and Clarence both rose to their feet. There were no stiff shoulders or cramps in the virtual world, but mental exhaustion still took a toll. They took their time, allowing movement to feel natural again.

Clarence and Pitohui waved their arms and hands in midair. They were calling up status windows to register each other as friends. Shirley scowled at the smiles on their faces, and when they were done, she muttered, "By the way, Pitohui..."

"What is it, Shirley?" she replied. It was a modicum of courtesy that they called each other by name.

"You leaked our information, didn't you?"

Clarence looked stunned. Pitohui asked, "What information?"

"You told people someone was lying in wait in the grass here, hoping to PK anyone who came by. No wonder we weren't seeing any targets!"

Pitohui said nothing. She only smiled. That was all the confirmation Shirley needed.

*   *   *

GOT TWO MORE MEMBERS! NOW WE'VE GOT A FULL SLATE OF SIX! said the message on the screen of the smartphone.

Yesssssss!

Miyu Shinohara threw her shoulders back and raised her arms to the sky, like a soccer player celebrating a spectacular goal. In her mind, at least.

In reality, she did no such thing, because she was on the train.

JR Hokkaido's Super Ozora was hurtling through the greenery of the mountains, its blue cars tilting to the side as the track curved. This was an express train that left Sapporo, ran through Obihiro—Miyu's home—and onward to the city of Kushiro.

Miyu was sitting in the window seat in the last row of an ordinary coach car. Around her in the box seats, which were flipped to face each other, were three teenage girls wearing plain clothes rather than school uniforms. Unlike Miyu, who had been hanging out in Sapporo yesterday, these girls seemed to be heading all the way to Kushiro.

They were having a great time chatting, the conversation rapidly flitting between topics like the upcoming school semester, their eventual college entrance exams, the programs that had aired online last night, a rumored boyfriend one of their friends had supposedly started seeing, and so on.

Outside the window, the sights of Hokkaido at the end of its short summer sped by. Fall would arrive soon, followed by the long winter, when the temperature would drop to around zero.

With the high school girls around her, Miyu focused on her smartphone and typed her response. Her fingers moved like lightning.

OH YEAH, BABY! SAWEET! YOU DA BEST! MY GOD! she typed.

The "message seen" receipt appeared immediately.

KNOCK IT OFF. I KNOW ALREADY, came the reply.

NO, YOU'RE EVEN MORE OF A GOD THAN YOU REALIZE!

OKAY, ENOUGH OF THAT. NOW IT'S YOUR TURN. IF YOU DON'T GET LLENN IN, YOU'RE IN BIG TROUBLE, YOU KNOW THAT? I'M GONNA KILL YOU. IN THE GAME.

I WILL DO MY BEST NOT TO INVOKE THE WRATH OF A GOD, Miyu typed. At that very moment, the teenage girls changed topics again.

"Isn't Elza Kanzaki's new song just the best?"

"Yeah, and she's awesome. It's so cool how she plays guitar and sings with that little body of hers."

"I wish I could be as beautiful and delicate as her," they said, utterly enraptured with the pop singer.

GOOD LUCK. I HAVE TO PREP FOR TONIGHT'S WORK. GOT A BIG DINNER MEETING WITH SOME DISGUSTING FATTY COMB-OVER HARASSING BALD-ASS DEATH-STENCH FREAK WHO'S A BIG SHOT AT A MAJOR PUBLISHER. REAL SUCK-ASS JOB, IF YOU ASK ME, said the message from the person on the other end.

Well, good luck to you, too, thought Miyu as she closed the messaging app. The contact name listed at the top of the chat window said GOD.

∗   ∗   ∗

Around the time Miyu was trading messages with the singing sensation she idolized, Karen Kohiruimaki was being introduced by her father.

"This is my youngest daughter, Karen."

Today, she wasn't dressed in her usual, low-key fashion of a shirt and pants, nor was she done up in *GGO*-style combat fatigues. In fact, she was wearing an elegant pale-blue party dress.

At this hour the day before, when buying the dress at the department store near the train station, the sales associate had gushed over her, saying, "Ma'am, you must be a model! I think almost anything would look good on you, so I'll bring a large selection!"

All she'd wanted to do was rush right out of the store, though.

Across from her was a man in his sixties, the same generation as her father. "Aaah! Is that you, Karen? I haven't seen you since you were a little girl, back in Hokkaido. And now you're…so… big," he said haltingly.

Now that she was trapped here with no way to escape an awkward situation, she wanted to run away even more.

She was standing in the glamorous reception hall of a famous luxury hotel in Tokyo. It was a hallowed, coveted space—the kind of room where celebrities held their wedding receptions.

Karen's father ran his own company, and his line of business held a yearly gathering of companies for social purposes. The party didn't have a fixed date each time, but this year it happened to be today, August 20th, at this location.

Her father took part in it every year, and so he traveled to Tokyo each time. Typically, Karen's mother would accompany him—she looked forward to an annual trip to the capital, too. But alas, a nasty summer flu had knocked her out this year.

When such things happened, one of Karen's two older sisters would be called upon to serve as a "replacement escort," but as luck would have it, both of them had firm prior engagements that kept them away.

That left Karen as the last option.

She'd been relaxing after her return to Tokyo when the news hit her like a shot out of the blue the morning before.

Why can't you just go and have fun with the guys?! she had raged internally, but there was no use complaining about a social world that didn't make sense in the first place.

She didn't hate her father, though, and didn't want him to be embarrassed, so she had no choice but to prop up the family business and take one for the team.

And precisely as she knew would happen…she stood out above the crowd.

There were hardly any Japanese women who were six feet tall. Among the elderly men and their wives was one young woman with Hollywood-actress height and slim proportions, done up with the makeup style her sister had forced her to learn. Her presence had enough impact to stop the conversations of all those wineglass-swirling old men as soon as they saw her.

"I'm so glad to have you here with me, Karen," said her doting father, clearly pleased that his youngest daughter was the center of attention. "Maybe I should have you come to all of these from now on," he suggested, smiling. The idea was so terrifying that it stimulated her fighting spirit, as if she were battling Pitohui and Boss.

"Okay, Dad. But I'll have to tell Mom, and I don't know if you'll survive to see the party next year…"

"Well, well… Look who's got a razor-sharp tongue…"

She didn't feel like threatening her father beyond that. Karen gave up and decided to wait it out until she could leave.

Fortunately, her father was as dedicated to his job as he was to his children, so once enough introductions had been made, he let her see to her own affairs and proceeded to engage in business talk with his industry peers.

Karen was twenty, of legal age, but didn't drink alcohol, so she ordered a grape juice. She sipped it, decided that a luxury hotel certainly did serve fine juice, then retreated to the side, leaning against the strangely patterned wall of the banquet area.

She glanced at the delicate wristwatch her sister lent her, so fragile it seemed likely to break at a single touch. About an hour remained of the party.

Karen found herself nostalgic about the display readout that Llenn wore as a watch in *GGO*. It made her wish that the AmuSphere could be as small as a pair of glasses so she could dive in right here.

One glance at her watch made it feel like her heart had just jumped into *GGO*—as if she'd gone from a giant in a dress to tiny, energetic, active Llenn. To her other self.

The last time she'd played was last Sunday, the sixteenth—the playtest.

She'd logged in with Miyu's extra AmuSphere at her friend's house, fought a bunch of powerful AI characters, and failed in various ways—but overall, it had been a very entertaining and fulfilling day.

When it was over, she'd spent time at the bar with M, Pito, and Fukaziroh, having a little party. In fact, at the time, Pitohui had said something about the fourth Squad Jam being announced and opening for enrollment soon.

Karen went back through her memories, realizing that all the twists and turns of Squad Jam had happened this very year, 2026.

The first was held on February 1st.

She'd fought with M on Pitohui's introduction, defeating the team of professionals, MMTM, and though there had been some personal difficulty at the end, they'd even overcome the mighty SHINC and won.

Up to that point, Llenn had only won PvP battles by sneaking up on people from behind, so it had been a valuable combat experience. It certainly gave her lots of confidence. She'd become friends with the gymnastics team from the high school affiliated with her college.

SJ2 was on April 4th.

M had begged Llenn to save Pitohui by killing her in the game, so the speedy pink girl had entered the competition with her trusty companion, Fukaziroh. They'd kicked a lot of ass, destroyed some annoying obstacles, and engaged in a stunning battle to the death with the wicked boss Pitohui at the end. All in all, it had been great fun.

After that, she'd met her favorite singer, Elza Kanzaki, in person, an encounter she would never forget for the rest of her life. Though she'd successfully forgotten about the kiss.

The last Squad Jam, SJ3, was on July 5th.

That was the first time she'd successfully teamed up with Pitohui. It was supposed to be her big chance to engage her age-old rivals, SHINC.

Unfortunately, because of a stupid rule that took a member from each team to form a new team of betrayers after a certain point in the game (a rule implemented by that goddamn writer—no, excuse me, let's clean that up a little—by that writer afflicted with serious personality issues) she'd gone through hell.

Of course, all's well that ends well. When it turned out that Boss was also a betrayer, she got to fight alongside her, which had been quite enjoyable in its own way.

So what would happen in SJ4?

SJ3 had been a moderate success, and given that she hadn't seen any obituaries for the author sponsoring the events, it seemed all but certain there would be another tournament.

Pitohui and M were speculating it might come as early as the start of next month or even the end of this one. Naturally, that transitioned into a discussion of what to do about their team lineup. Should they go in as the four-person LPFM team again? Or should they recruit another two to fill out the roster?

The best regular teams in Squad Jam were getting tougher all the time, especially ZEMAL, the All-Japan Machine-Gun Lovers. The gymnastics team (SHINC) and Memento Mori (MMTM) were sharpening their claws, too, waiting for the opportunity to avenge their prior defeats.

The thought of going in as a four-man team was a bit intimidating now. Their rivals would certainly be trying to maximize their manpower, for one thing.

But which two players would be both capable enough to add something to the team and agreeable enough to deal with a group full of powerful, eccentric personalities? Llenn couldn't think of anyone right off the bat.

At the time, Pitohui'd had a scheming expression on her face, but then again, she always looked that way. Of course, that's because she *was* scheming. But Karen decided not to think too hard about it.

"Need something to do?"

It took someone speaking to her directly to pull Karen's mind back out of distant *GGO*. She craned her neck to the right toward the voice and saw no one. Just more of the banquet hall, same as before.

Oh? She could have sworn she'd heard a man's voice. Was she hearing things now?

"Now look down," said the same voice, from very close by.

"Mmm?"

She tilted her head down, lowering her field of view. At last, she saw the man. He was right in front of her—and had been there the entire time.

"I'm pretty small, aren't I?"

He was right. He was so short, she'd failed to spot him. In fact, he was barely five feet tall, nearly as short as Llenn in *GGO*. He was also notably wide, so he seemed as round as an egg.

He didn't seem to be in his twenties or his forties, so she guessed he was thirty-something by process of elimination. Like all the other men at this party, he wore an expensive-looking suit, and his short hair was slicked firmly back with gel.

The man beamed, his face as round as his body. "I've always had a complex about my appearance, being so short and round. People have laughed at me my entire life. I've always lamented why I had to be born small and fat," he said, a surprisingly frank admission. "Are you going to laugh at me, too?"

It all came in a rush. His voice was gentle, but the look in his eyes was deadly serious.

"No," she said immediately. "I've always been laughed at for being tall, so I would never make fun of someone else for a body type they can't do anything about."

That was her honest opinion. She knew exactly how much she'd been mocked and scorned by others and would never forget that, which was why Karen would never do the same to someone in a similar situation. That was a promise she wouldn't break to her dying day.

The man grinned again. "I'm glad I spoke to you, then. Nice to meet you. My name is Fire Nishiyamada."

"Huh?"

Karen's mind froze. He'd said something, but it certainly didn't sound like a name.

The man's smile never faded, as though he'd anticipated her reaction and enjoyed it. "When you write my surname in kanji, it means 'paddy on the western mountain.' And my given name is the kanji for *fire*, but pronounced like the English word. It's pretty wild, huh? Basically no one at school or work has ever read it properly on the first try!"

Well, of course they haven't, Karen thought. With the ice broken now, though, she no longer had any innate resistance to talking to this man named Nishiyamada.

"I'm Karen Kohiruimaki. It's written with the kanji for *fragrant lotus*, and my last name is *small*, *comparison*, *type*, and *wrap*. People often tell me that my family name is exotic."

The list of descriptions for the kanji for her name was a

sequence she'd been saying since she was a child to introduce herself to others. Miyu said it was cool because it sounded like something an idol singer would say.

All young women, not just Karen, would be cautious around an unfamiliar man, but as this was a gathering of her father's industry peers, everyone here was accountable in some way. She felt safe enough to give her name without worrying about it being used against her.

"Kohiruimaki is a name you see a lot in the city of Misawa in Aomori Prefecture. Are you from there?"

"Yes, my father is. I was born and raised in Obihiro, Hokkaido."

"Obihiro, Hokkaido! I've been there a number of times! I know it's famous for its pork bowls, but I happen to really like the local chain's curry! What about you, Karen?"

"Oh, I went there all the time in high school with my friends."

"You did? Boy, it would be great to have that every day. I also remember that huge temperature gauge outside of Obihiro Station..."

Well, well! Nishiyamada was equipped with quite the conversational skill. His knowledge was impressive. He knew a lot about Karen's native Hokkaido and kept the small talk moving without getting awkward.

Certainly, anyone watching their interaction would think, *What a friendly little odd couple they make!* After all, they were at least a foot apart in height. Judging by profile alone, they could have been mother and son.

In the end, they talked for about fifteen minutes. There was nothing particularly noteworthy in their conversation, and when it was over, Karen couldn't even be sure what they had talked about. It had, however, been a good way to pass the time.

In fact, it was the first chance she'd had to talk with a young man outside of her family since Goushi, right before SJ2. What if this was the initiation of a pickup attempt? What if he started asking for contact information?

The thought made Karen wary again, but Nishiyamada simply

said, "Oops, I ought to say hello to some other people now. Sorry," and withdrew without bothering her further.

On that cue, Karen worried *this* might be the moment he tried to ask for her information and tensed again, but all the little round man named Fire said was, "Well, so long. This was fun," and then he promptly turned and left. He slipped through the men in the party around them and was out of sight.

Phew. I didn't get hit on, Karen thought, relieved. But before long…

"Oh…I'd be careful around that guy," cautioned Miyu over the phone later that night.

Miyu's voice sounded echoey over the smartphone's speaker while she took a bath in her family's house. She had a habit of taking long baths for her beauty and health, and she usually called Karen during them because she got bored and had nothing else to do.

After they'd talked about Karen's dress, which Miyu insisted on getting a picture of, Karen brought up the topic of Nishiya-mada, at which point Miyu delivered that warning.

"Careful…? What do you mean?"

"I mean that he's absolutely got his eye on you, Kohi. You can't help it; you're a far more appealing woman than you realize. It's the fate of women like *us*—you just have to accept it," Miyu said, emphasizing that she was included in that category. Karen was too overwhelmed by the idea to comment on that part.

"But, but, but…all we did was waste a little time chatting. He didn't even ask for my number," she protested, shaking her head. Her smartphone was resting on the charging stand next to the bed, where she lay facedown.

"You can't be too careful. What'd you say this guy's name was, Fire? He's going to fill the moat from the outside. You remember the summer campaign of the Siege of Osaka, right? That's right…it was a hot and moist day…"

"Stop acting like you were there four hundred years ago. What do you mean?"

"The fact that he didn't ask you for your information directly is because he knows he can get it other ways. He works in your dad's industry, right? All he has to do is ask around about 'Kohirui-maki from Obihiro,' and he'll get all he needs."

"Oh…"

That was a good point. Everyone there had each other's information saved, of course. But what kind of man would have any interest in a beanpole of a woman like her? Karen thought it was too unlikely.

Then Miyu said cryptically, "But you know, it's not a bad thing to have a man's interest."

"Huh? What makes you say that?"

"Maybe the time is right for you to try dating someone, Kohi."

"What? Why should I?"

"Maybe you and Fire will turn out to be the perfect couple. Who knows?"

"But… I'm saying…"

"Call me when you have the wedding planned. And if you need tips on dating etiquette, I can help you out."

"Ummm…excuse meee…"

"By the way, if there's an SJ4, are you gonna play with everyone?"

"Huh? Well, um, sure," Karen admitted. The question came so suddenly that she gave her answer without thinking.

"Excellent! Well, I recorded this whole conversation, so now I gotta send the file over to Pito!"

"Wait, was that all you wanted…?" Karen asked, aghast. Miyu didn't care about the stuff with Nishiyamada at all.

"That's right. Pito threatened me, saying I had to drag Llenn into the next Squad Jam or she'd kill me! Open parentheses, inside of *GGO*, close parentheses. And you know… I value my life… I'm still so young…so beautiful…"

"Yeah, right. I bet you were happy to oblige her."

"Oh, I didn't know you were psychic."

The topic of Nishiyamada had completely left Karen's mind by now. Mentally speaking, she was back in the wastelands of *GGO*.

"The next Squad Jam... This time, this time for sure...I'm going to settle the score with Saki and the gymnastics team...," she murmured, closing her eyes. She envisioned the sturdy silhouettes of Team SHINC.

In the midst of them, she saw a gorilla-like woman with braided pigtails, holding the terrifying Vintorez silenced sniper rifle and wearing a smile that would make small children scream and run.

"Yes. That's the spirit... Go on...fight, you tiny pink devil... Spill the CG blood of your enemies... Your heart...your throat thirsts for blood..."

"Ewww! Stop dubbing in creepy narration, Miyu!"

"Wah-ha-ha-ha-ha! Anyway, let's have fun in the next Squad Jam! Guess I should get out now. Thanks for helping me kill time."

"Sure. Let me know if they announce it," Karen said in closing. That was the end of her enjoyable chat with Miyu. "And now I should take a bath myself and go to bed!"

She had no way of knowing what would happen to her the following day.

Friday, August 21st. Morning.

The fourth Squad Jam was announced, and registration opened for all teams.

At nearly the same time, Karen's father received a message from Nishiyamada that read:

I would like to formally begin a relationship with Karen, with an eye toward our eventual marriage.

CHAPTER 2
The Man Named Fire

SECT.2

CHAPTER 2
The Man Named Fire

Hey, all you gun freaks squatting in GGO! How ya been?

I'm good, by the way! Good enough to announce a fourth installment of the Squad Jam series! I'm talking about SJ4!

Let's get together and fight next Wednesday, August 26th, at noon!

The usual Squad Jam sponsor's message was as flippant as ever.

If memory served correctly, he was fifty-four years old, but he wrote like a child. It was almost laughable, in a sad way.

The message came with the title: *Announcing SJ4 and Open Registration.* Every player who had ever competed in a Squad Jam received it at 10:00 AM on August 21st.

"Let's goooooooooooooooooooooo!" screamed Saki Nitobe, the player of Eva (aka Boss), leader of SHINC, as she sat at the table eating a late breakfast at home during summer vacation. Her mother scolded her fiercely for that one.

"No phones at the table!" she snapped. Saki put all her concentration into finishing her breakfast. She was having French toast, but in her mind, she was already in a one-on-one battle with Llenn.

How should I beat her? How should I kill her? she wondered.

Currently, the gymnastics team was in trouble, as they hadn't gained any new first-year members. The team captain, however, didn't seem particularly concerned about it for now.

David, the leader of MMTM, had a day off from his job as a delivery truck driver, so he'd been playing *GGO* from early in the morning, practicing his shooting by himself.

He noticed a blinking signal in the corner of his vision indicating a new message and paused in the act of firing his Steyr STM-556 assault rifle so he could wave his left hand and bring up the player menu.

"Ha-ha-ha!"

He read the header and laughed. Then he emptied the rest of his magazine with a smile on his face. Every last bullet vanished into the human-shaped target five hundred feet down the shooting range lane.

"Just you wait, Pitohui!"

He, too, was wondering, *How should I beat her? How should I kill her?*

The rules will be essentially unchanged from the last time, and the seeding and preliminary rounds will work the same way. Nothing big will change.

This will be the schedule for each step of SJ4. All of these dates are in August.

Monday the twenty-fourth, 9:00 PM, is the entry deadline.

Tuesday the twenty-fifth, 12:00 PM, is the start of the preliminary round.

Wednesday the twenty-sixth, 12:00 PM, is the start of the main event.

How-ev-er!

There will be another set of special rules for SJ4! Very special rules!

*   *   *

Nearly every player reading the message at that point thought, *Ugh, not again! Give it a rest! Just because you're the sponsor doesn't mean you should abuse your sponsor's privileges!*

But not all of them were fuming.

The woman who played Pitohui, the popular singer-songwriter Elza Kanzaki, was wrapped up in the sheets atop her large bed, completely nude, AC turned to downright frigid in her bedroom.

Outside the window was a forest of Tokyo high-rises. The image of bright sunlight shining through lace curtains onto a black-haired beauty resting on white sheets was stunningly artistic.

Any Elza fan who witnessed such a sexy and beautiful sight might die of shock.

There was a large monitor on the wall of the bedroom. The sight of the words on the screen made her grin with demonic glee. "Ooh, I can't wait! What kind of ridiculous rule is it going to be this time?!"

"I'm coming in," said Goushi Asougi as he entered the bedroom with a cup of hot black coffee and offered it to Elza.

"Thank you," she said as she took it and lifted it quietly to her lips.

Incidentally, Goushi was wearing an apron and nothing else. He was bare-assed naked.

"Mmm, delicious. Turn around. Here's your reward."

Elza wound up and kicked his bare ass hard.

Any Elza fan who witnessed such a violent and beautiful sight might die of shock.

But rest assured—it won't be the Betrayer rule from SJ3!

It's no fun doing the same things all over again! Nobody likes a writer who runs out of ideas!

So this time, I won't be splitting up any team that shares a bond of blood and friendship!

SJ4's going to be a hardcore battle royale, designed to determine the best team of all!

*   *   *

At that point, Huey, the rooster-headed member of Team ZEMAL, screeched, "The hell you say! We ain't bound by something wimpy *everyone* shares, like blood! We're connected by frickin' belt links!"

It was an odd thing to get worked up about. A belt link is the piece of metal that strings together the ammo a machine gun uses. The problem is, those tear apart into individual pieces once the bullets are fired, but we don't need to point that out to him, do we?

Huey stood there, massive M240B machine gun in his hands, as his four nearby companions murmured and nodded to themselves. Once again, they were having fun playing *GGO* on a weekday morning. Several members of the team had jobs. Apparently, that no longer mattered.

When they noticed the messages, they all called up their menus and began reading atop the rocky mountain in the sun. They were wearing their usual team uniform: green fleece jackets with their logo, and black combat pants.

Each member carried his own machine gun with a special rail attached that ran around his side to a large backpack. This was their "backpack ammo-loading system," which they used to great effect in the playtest last week, allowing them to fire up to a thousand bullets consecutively.

Now that they were completely distracted by the message about SJ4, a giant black bearlike monster snuck up on them, almost entirely silent. This area was dotted with boulders the size of trucks, which limited visibility. It was the perfect place for a surprise attack on unsuspecting prey.

The bear crouched down behind a large rock. It was ready to pounce on its five-course meal.

Whoosh! Without so much as a roar, the bear pounced with all its might, launching itself into the air over one of the rocks.

It was a tremendous jump, spanning a good thirty feet. The bear's sharp claws were extended, and it plunged into ZEMAL's midst…

Dak-gak-gak-gak-gak-gak-gak-gak-gak-gak-gak-gak!

A single gun fired. A stream of bullets pierced the huge bear's body as it descended. Only a machine gun could do that much damage so quickly.

"Hah!" "Mmm!" "Fwah?" "Oh?" "Whut?"

The five men were stunned—to them, a giant beast, its body glowing red with damage spots, had appeared out of thin air, plummeting to the ground and slamming between them. The corpse quickly dispersed into particles and vanished.

The members of ZEMAL stood there, openmouthed in shock.

Though they'd nearly been eaten by a ferocious monster in their carelessness, they *did* have enough self-awareness to realize that someone else had saved them.

From atop a nearby rock came a high-pitched voice.

"Hi there! That was a close one!"

It was a woman's voice. A soprano.

The five looked up with a start.

"But thanks to that, I got an easy kill! Lucky me! What a prize!"

Standing about twenty yards away was a woman they'd never seen before. Her avatar seemed to be about twenty years old.

She had fine facial features and pure, flawless skin. Her gray eyes were impossibly deep, her wine-red hair was cut short and fine, and there was a dark-blue beanie resting over it.

She was short and petite, though not to the extent of that pink shrimp. She wore a jacket and tiger-striped pants in shades of green. In her hands, she held the weapon that had riddled the giant bear with bullets only a moment ago...

"An RPD!"

"With a short-barrel alteration!"

ZEMAL's love for machine guns was no joke; they recognized it at once.

The weapon she had slung from her shoulder was an old Soviet machine gun called an RPD. It was a light machine gun that used the same ammunition as an AK-47.

The slim design made it lightweight to begin with, and she had modified it from there. She'd severed the long barrel and taken off the heavy bipod, making the gun even lighter and more mobile. There were records of American special forces making similar customizations to this gun during the Vietnam War.

From their first glance, this woman with the fancy, customized machine gun was the picture of ZEMAL's collective ideal.

Their hearts were swept away. It took only an instant.

A beauty carrying a machine gun. Wouldn't that make her... our goddess?

I mean, she has to be. There's no reason she wouldn't be.

This is the goddess sent to us by the god of machine guns.

It was already a system of faith for them. Five true believers had been born in no time.

Faced with five men making the stupidest faces imaginable, the woman added, "Oh, you're the machine-gun team that plays in Squad Jam, right? I saw you on the video." Her voice was kind and gentle and friendly and beautiful.

Oh! She knows who we are! What a gift—what an honor. Their newfound faith was stronger than ever.

"But you know, you guys are terrible at strategy. You've got the most firepower by far, but it feels like you're wasting it."

Ooh! Our goddess speaks! They continued to worship.

"If you utilized more strategy, you could easily get into the top ranks, even win the entire thing, I think."

"In that case—!" shouted black-haired Shinohara. "Please join our team and lead us as you see fit!"

Instantly, all five of the men took a knee. It was a pristine and unified motion, though no one had telegraphed the move.

The burly men lowered their heads to the beautiful woman standing atop the rock. She was wide-eyed initially.

"Pfft! Ah-ha-ha-ha-ha! Ah-ha-ha-ha-ha-ha-ha-ha!"

She burst into surprised, extended laughter. Her voice was quick and sharp, like automatic gunfire in the wasteland of wind and bullets or the singing of an angel. The pleasure it elicited in the men was as satisfying as if their hit points had just been recovered in full.

Once her laughter subsided, the machine-gunning beauty said, "All right! I'll join your team!"

"Reallyyyyyyyy?!" the five screamed. It was loud enough to shake the earth or knock out nearby monsters.

"I'm not a liar. You're going to play in the next Squad Jam, I assume? That sounds fun! I'll be the leader, and I'll turn you into the toughest bunch in the game!"

The men shouted and bellowed. They were mad with delight. They danced; they cried; they prayed.

In fact, they seemed to have completely forgotten to read the rules of SJ4.

As the five men cavorted around her like children, the woman mumbled, "Ummm...isn't anyone going to ask what my name is?"

As a matter of fact, yet again the special rules are going to remain a secret until the game begins! But you'll figure it out right away once you start! Look forward too it, everyone!

Not only was the writer's tone annoying, he'd also made a typo. He'd clearly meant to say "look forward to it." That was something a proofreader would have to fix in a novel. How had he not caught that?

But I'll let you in on a little secret right now!

I have two very special announcements about these special rules! And they're very important, so read them carefully!

First of all, I'm allowing automatic refilling of ammunition! In SJ4, after thirty minutes have passed, all the ammo each player has used (bullets, energy charges for optical guns and photon swords, hand grenades) will be replenished!

But no damage done to weapons or armor will be repaired.

And as for character HP, you only get the three emergency med kits, like usual.

There will be similar refills at the one-hour, hour-thirty, and two-hour marks as well, so use your ammunition freely.

Because if you don't...oops! I can't finish that sentence for you yet.

"What's that supposed to mean...?" Ervin wondered out loud.

He was a member of Team T-S, the group of sci-fi soldiers wearing futuristic armor. They were seeded because they had taken advantage of circumstances to steal the win in SJ2.

Ervin was the one with the number 002 on his helmet who had been labeled the betrayer in SJ3, so he'd fought alongside Pitohui atop the luxury cruise ship. She was also the one who'd killed him in the end.

In last week's playtest, T-S had worked with the other teams and made good use of their defensive capability to stand in the lead.

They were currently assembled in a ruined city, surrounded by partially collapsed buildings. It looked like the end of the world, and there was a subset of people who loved that vibe.

Nearby, his other teammates, who were distinguishable only by their numbers, sounded equally suspicious.

"Is he saying that's how fierce the battle's going to be?"

"I'd say the previous ones have been pretty fierce already. There were some people running out of ammo by the end in the past, right?"

"Exactly... So why is this one going to feature full ammo replenishing?"

"I don't know. I don't understand *anything* that goes through that writer's head..."

Ervin chose to be positive. "Well, it's nice to have all your ammo come back. It means you can shoot as much as you want. Let's kick some butt." He knew from past experience that no one could predict what was going to happen in Squad Jam.

Dealing with Pitohui had made everyone tougher.

And here's the second part!

This time, every single player's going to bring a pistol!

Why? Because a truly excellent GGO player needs to have mastery over all kinds of weapons. There are going to be multiple areas on this map where no weapons aside from pistols are allowed.

Any non-pistol firearm will be automatically locked and unable to fire in those places. All you'll be able to use are pistols, knives, photon swords, hand grenades, and physical blows.

A pistol is defined as any weapon listed under the handgun category on its item properties window. You can use an ultratiny gun like a derringer or a big whopping S&W M500! Just know that you can't use a modified rifle with the barrel and stock shortened, like some kind of mobster gun.

Don't normally use a handgun? I have a bit of assistance for you!

For this event only, pistols, their holsters, magazines, and ammo will not count toward your character's weight limit. In other words, you can bring all of your usual gear and add the pistols for free! If you use pistols as part of your regular repertoire, you'll have room for more weapons!

Of course…if you don't want to bring them, that's your prerogative! Heh…

"Whaaat?"

Karen was reading the message on her notebook computer in her apartment in Tokyo, and she was not happy with these custom rules.

As Llenn, Karen had never actually used a handgun.

She got a lesson in shooting basics from the foulmouthed drill sergeant in the game's tutorial soon after starting *GGO*. However, using handguns didn't really click for her, and in the end, she'd stopped carrying a pistol.

The only gun she needed was P-chan, her P90 submachine gun. She could already shoot it with one hand like a pistol anyway. And the only sidearm she needed was her combat knife, Kni-chan. Plus the occasional grenade.

That was Llenn's style, and it had a track record of success. Now she was supposed to add a pistol she couldn't fire with any accuracy? What was the point?

"I guess I don't need one…," Karen decided. She looked up at the silent lights hanging from the ceiling of her bedroom and thought.

Pistols had a surprisingly short range as combat weapons. Even the best shot with a pistol couldn't hit a target farther than fifty yards away. Realistically, the range was even shorter if both sides were on the move.

There were times when two people firing handguns could pass just one or two dozen feet away and still fail to produce a fatality. At that rate, Llenn had enough speed that she could fight with only her knife.

In fact, when she fought Boss in the first Squad Jam, the other woman had had a pistol, and Llenn only a knife. And it had turned out all right in the end for her.

"All right! I don't need it!" Karen concluded neatly.

"Whaaat?"

Shirley was reading the message from her status window inside of *GGO*, and she was not happy with these custom rules.

She was in a rental space inside the game's capital city, SBC Glocken. It was a small room—about the size of a karaoke box—that could be borrowed for free. This was where she always made her exploding bullets. They were her secret weapon, her surefire one-hit kill rounds.

To Shirley's real-life player, Mai Kirishima, a hunter and nature guide in Hokkaido, summer was the busy season, when tourists seeking bountiful nature came to the northern island for guided experiences.

But on this day, she coincidentally had no engagements, so she was working on her ammo nice and early when the SJ4 announcement arrived. It was something she'd been anticipating, so it made her happy.

But like Llenn, Shirley wondered, "Pistols are required...?"

She'd started *GGO* to help practice her hunting skills. All Shirley needed was a bolt-action like her hunting rifle. Like Llenn, she hadn't touched a pistol since the tutorial.

"..."

She also had a knife at her side, the ken-nata. If she could use that in close quarters like she had when she'd fought Clarence...

"Dammit! That's not good enough!" Shirley spat, shaking her head.

If she fought, she fought to win. The whole point was to beat that hateful Pitohui.

Unfortunately, Pitohui was a crack shot with a pistol. She'd taken out Shirley's fleeing teammates in SJ2 with one-handed headshots, which was about the least stable and least reliable way to shoot. That said something about her skill.

The thought of taking on an opponent like that with nothing but a ken-nata just wasn't realistic. She had to acquire a pistol immediately and start practicing. Furthermore, if possible, she should make some exploding pistol rounds, too.

Then the face of the person she'd once fought popped into her head—a person who had an incredible quick-draw move. A person smiling, unbidden.

Shirley waved her left hand, hit a few buttons on her menu, then typed a message to someone registered as her in-game friend and sent it.

Hey, you're good with pistols, right?

Maybe! I'll help you buy one! Where you at? replied Clarence within seconds.

"Am I packing heat? Oh, you bet I got my piece on me..."

Miyu was standing in the middle of a crowded bus when she

announced that after reading the message. She nearly got the cops called on her.

Automatic ammo refills every thirty minutes and obligatory pistol use.

Keep these two elements in mind when you prepare for SJ4, everyone!

Registration is open from now until nine o'clock in the evening on Monday the twenty-fourth!

Step right up and try your luck!

✻   ✻   ✻

Karen had just finished reading the annoyingly informal invitation message when an Elza Kanzaki song began playing on her buzzing smartphone.

Few people knew her number—no one outside her family, Miyu, and Saki's group. Obviously, Miyu was the most frequent of those callers by far, so coming immediately after the announcement of SJ4, this one caught her unawares.

In other words, she lifted her phone to her ear without checking the caller ID and said, "Yeah, yeah, I read it."

"You read what?" asked her father. Karen nearly dropped her smartphone.

"Aaah—! Dad…? I'm sorry. I thought you were Miyu."

"Oh? What did you read, then?"

"…It's a secret."

"All right…fine. Good morning, Karen. Do you have a moment?"

It was very rare for her father to call her directly, so she shut her laptop. After yesterday's party, he'd presumably flown back home on the earliest flight this morning.

"Sure, what is it, Dad?"

He wasn't going to ask her to join him for another party, was he? Guilt-trip her by saying she'd already bought the dress, so what was the harm in attending another…?

She was prepared for the worst. Instead, to her great surprise, he said, "Karen, do you know someone named Fire Nishiyamada?"

Karen had no response.

He continued, "Fire is his actual name. Written with the kanji for *fire* but pronounced like the English word. Very strange name."

Huh? she thought before replying, "I know him... I talked with him for a few minutes at the party."

"Oh? And what is he like?"

"Umm...he's short. And...he didn't make fun of my height."

"Ah yes. He's well known in our business for his name and stature. A very promising young man—smart, proactive, and hardworking."

"Oh...I see..." Karen was starting to feel a little worried.

"Well, as a matter of fact, he just got in touch with me this morning."

"Wh...what did he say?" she asked. Her apprehension increased.

"He said, 'I would like to formally begin a relationship with Karen, with an eye toward our eventual marriage.'"

He's filling in the moat! Karen's mind was now trapped inside Osaka Castle.

"..."

"Hellooo? Karen?"

"...Wh...wh...wh...?"

"Should I give you a minute to calm down?" her father asked gently. Karen decided to take him up on that offer.

"Yes, please do... Give me ten years, in fact..."

"Well, I can't do that. It wouldn't be fair to him."

"Wh-why is this happening? How did this...?"

"It would be a long story," said her father, but he explained it all from the start.

An e-mail directed to his work address had arrived. In very clear terms, the message explained that its sender had met Karen at the party, was very smitten with her, and wanted to marry her.

"That's it."

"That was short! It wasn't long at all! S-so what did you tell him?"

"Well, that's why I'm calling you. To find out. Because how you feel is the most important thing."

"A-a-a-a-a-a-a..."

"Affirmative?"

"A-a-a..."

"A-OK?"

"Absolutely not! Why marriage what is that about I can't just go out with him what country do you think this is that makes no sense!" she erupted, nearly crushing the smartphone in her grip.

"Hmmm. So that's a no, then?"

"What do *you* think, Dad? I'm only twenty! I'm still in school!"

"Well...can I answer honestly?"

"Ugh... Okay."

"If you ask me, it's not a bad idea. I know he's a man who's used his complex about his short stature as motivation and found success. I feel like his struggles are similar to yours in that sense. I think he's someone who would understand your pain rather than merely sympathize or pity you for it."

"Ugh... But...I'm still—"

"I'm not done yet. Plus, it's not easy to say something like 'I'd like to start a relationship with an eye toward marriage.' That means he's already thinking about the responsibility involved. He's not asking on a mere whim. That's a very worthy thing. I don't think I could do that..."

Karen felt like that last comment probably deserved closer scrutiny, but she chose not to pursue it at this time.

"But of course, it's ultimately up to you, Karen. What do you think?"

"So you gave the okay, right, Kohi?"

"I said no!"

This time she really was on the phone with Miyu.

As soon as the call with her father ended, Karen had gotten off the bus outside Obihiro Station and rang her.

"He really was filling in the moat! I was shocked! And Dad was all for the idea—what's that about?! I can't believe this!" Karen ranted.

Miyu said calmly, "Yeah, but I kind of understand where your dad is coming from... He's much older than my parents. I mean, you're his youngest daughter, so which guy is he going to prefer—some nobody out of nowhere or a man whose qualifications he already knows from work? It's pretty simple."

"I...I'm not denying the logic!"

"And you did talk with him, at least for a few minutes, right? Did you find him gross or unpleasant?"

"N-no, I didn't think so!"

"So if you don't dislike him, what's wrong with going out with him?"

"Marriage is way off! I'm not thinking about it now at all!"

"But you want to do it someday, right? I didn't think you were the lifelong single type. You said you wanted to have a normal marriage and family, right?"

"Th-that's true...," murmured Karen, cooling off after a conversation of unbroken exclamation points.

She had a desire to get married in the future, as much as the average person did. Her two older sisters had happy marriages and children, and they seemed to be enjoying their lives. It struck her as only natural that she should want the same.

"Then why don't you try snagging a man who shows interest from the start? What's his name, Fire? Was he not your type?"

"Huh? I don't know..."

"What *is* your type, Kohi? It doesn't hurt to say. Go on."

Karen felt like Miyu was going to make fun of her no matter what the answer was, so it absolutely *would* hurt to say, but she went ahead and told the truth.

"Someone like P-chan..."

"That's not a man. C'mon, at least make it a human being... What are you going to do, marry a gun?"

"I-it's just an example! I mean, someone who's reliable, has high specs, a good design..."

"Fine, fine, fine. Well, if you're not interested, then I guess you don't need to force yourself to go along with it."

Wow, Miyu gave up on that one very easily, Karen thought, relieved.

"So introduce him to me instead. I don't care if he's short or fat—maybe I'll think he's cute when I get used to him. Appearance isn't what men are about. The biggest draw of all is if he's rich!"

"…"

"Then I'll give him one date. I'm sure he'll take me out to some swanky sushi place in Ginza! And I've been looking forward to getting a new bag! And if I'm really pushing it, a brand-new car. Ooh, I want a car! Like a Benz or a BMW!"

Karen had a sudden urge to go back through her memories and figure out exactly *why* she was friends with Miyu.

"And if you want, Kohi, you can watch us having a hot and heavy date, from far away or even up close—I don't care!"

"Why…would I do that?"

"Hey, maybe you'll come around to seeing the finer side of young Fire. Have you ever heard these famous, ancient words? 'When a man is single, a woman looks for reasons he can't be her boyfriend.'"

"Uh-huh."

"And the second part goes, 'But when she sees a man getting along with another woman, she looks for reasons she could have him for herself.'"

"You argued this one pretty passionately before, didn't you? Basically, that the definition of a hot man is a man other women want."

"That's it. In other words, if I go on a date with Fire, you're going to try to see his best qualities! So do I have the green light to date him? Do I?"

It sounded as though Miyu was trying to peer into her mind.

"Yeah, sure," said Karen in all honestly. Then she added, "Can we talk about SJ4 now?"

＊   ＊   ＊

Sunday, August 23rd. Midday.

At a table in a pub in *GGO*'s capital city, SBC Glocken, four people were seated: Llenn, in pink; Fukaziroh, in brown; Pitohui, in navy blue; and M, in green. Aside from them, the place was empty, so they didn't need a private room. They occupied a booth for four along the aisle of the pub.

It was a simple teatime gathering, under the guise of the team's first meeting since Friday's announcement of SJ4.

"Thanks for showing up. The other two weren't able to make it today," said Pitohui, right as she arrived. Across from her, Llenn sipped her iced tea.

"The other two?" she asked. "Are we going as a team of six this time, Pito?"

Pitohui's face suddenly darkened with alarm. "Llenn…can you…read my mind…?"

"It was really obvious from the way you said it! So who are they…?" Llenn asked, half worried and half excited.

Having a full team of six for Squad Jam would be a major boost to their power, but she couldn't help worrying about what might happen if they didn't click. Putting aside the question of whether Pitohui clicked with the rest of the team in the first place, of course.

"You've heard of them before, actually. It's Clarence and Shirley," Pitohui explained.

Llenn and Fukaziroh were stunned.

"Really…?"

"No frickin' way!"

Fukaziroh knew about the plan to recruit more members but hadn't been told who the candidates were earlier.

Clarence and Shirley. Llenn knew those names.

Clarence was the person who'd given up her P90 magazines in SJ2 when Llenn threatened—er, negotiated with her, for the price of a kiss.

Shirley was a very dangerous sniper who'd shot Pitohui from long distance in SJ2 and very nearly killed her. In SJ3, she used deadly explosive rounds and phenomenal aim to dispatch a number of unlucky victims.

As a matter of fact, those two had engaged in one hell of a battle in SJ3. Llenn had found that out when she'd watched the replay of the event with Saki and the girls.

When Karen saw the clip of Shirley driving the ken-nata into Clarence's stomach, she'd grunted and turned her eyes away from it. Saki, who'd had her throat cut by Llenn while playing as Boss, just glared at her accusingly.

Fukaziroh asked, "Well, this is a big surprise, Pito, but how did you convince them to join? They seem like the two players least likely to join us."

"They must have been struck by my vehement passion."

"Not struck by your violent bullets?"

"A few of those, too."

In the meantime, Llenn was thinking hard about their team balance.

She was a frontline attacker, someone who moved fast, scouting ahead and striking quickly. She was small and hard to hit but couldn't take much damage. The P90's maximum effective range wasn't much more than six hundred feet, less than half that of an assault rifle, and its bullets were relatively weak.

Clarence was probably similar in build for offense. Her AR-57 used the same ammo as the P90, so her range was somewhere in the same neighborhood.

According to the stats that Llenn had glimpsed on her menu during SJ2, though, Clarence was slower than Llenn, with much higher stamina and strength. She must have played the game a whole lot.

M was the tough guy, of course. He was excellent at sniping with his M14 EBR, and his fierce physical stamina and powerful shield gave him very high defense. He could drive any working vehicle, and he calmly and intelligently gave orders under fire.

Fukaziroh had unparalleled firepower with her pair of six-shooter grenade launchers, which made her a very valuable support member. She was as tiny as Llenn but far hardier in terms of stamina. The only point of concern was her propensity for going rogue from time to time.

Pitohui could skillfully use a variety of guns and swords, and you could count on her to win almost any kind of battle aside from a long-distance one. She had very high health as well. She was a monster—a demon lord. Terrifying. The last person you wanted to fight. Thank goodness she wasn't on the enemy's side.

Shirley was an incredible sniper, capable of shooting distant targets without a bullet line, and thanks to her explosive rounds, any hit was a guaranteed fatal shot.

"Dang…isn't this lineup kind of…amazing? Our team is really balanced now!" Llenn observed. She was delighted.

"Right? LPFMSC is going to be the best squad in the competition! The dream team!" said Pitohui, her smile distorting her cheek tattoos.

Squishing in two more initials into the team name only made it harder to say, but no one soured the mood by pointing that out. Besides, team abbreviations could only go up to five letters, so it wouldn't fly in Squad Jam. They'd need to come up with something else.

All that aside, Llenn's mind was filled with one thought: *I can do it this time! I can fight SHINC head-on and compete with them!* Having a full team of six was a dream come true for her.

She'd always assumed she and M had beaten the girls in SJ1 by sheer luck.

To have a proper rematch against SHINC, she needed a powerful team around her first. Even if that ultimately resulted in defeat.

And if this group of six participated in SJ4, they were going to try to win it all.

That meant that somewhere along the way, they'd have to run up against SHINC. Saki had already messaged her as if it was only natural they would be playing, too.

"I'm so happy. I might be more excited about this Squad Jam than any of the others... Just you wait, Boss!" Llenn exclaimed, as happy as a child, sipping her iced tea in delighted anticipation.

"..."

M silently elbowed Pitohui in the side. His expression imparted some kind of meaning, like he wanted to say something or have her say something.

"..."

But Pitohui was silent, pretending she didn't notice.

She wasn't going to tell Llenn that Shirley and Clarence were only joining the team as a means of bypassing the preliminary round. Once SJ4 started, Pitohui had agreed they were free to pursue their individual agendas.

"Well, now that we've finished the team's bonding ceremony, what about the rest of the day? Wanna go slaughter some pitiable monsters or players?" Pitohui suggested, though it didn't sound like a joke. Other people might walk past their table, so it would be nice if she didn't chat openly about PKing.

"Yeah! Let's kill 'em!" added Fukaziroh. Very violent, very disruptive.

Speaking of Fukaziroh, she'd converted her character over from her main haunt, the fantasy game *ALfheim Online*, for the playtest on the sixteenth and had been hanging out in *GGO* since then.

PKing aside, Llenn thought it was a good opportunity to get into a tough battle and shoot her P-chan a whole bunch. She drained the rest of her iced tea and stood up at her full, mostly insignificant height.

"Okay, let's go!"

At that very moment, a man approached her from behind and said, "Hello, Karen Kohiruimaki!"

Karen was so shocked that she thought the software might boot her right out.

The sudden greeting was bad enough, but what made it far worse was that the person used her real name.

In the virtual world, full-dive or not, referring to someone by their real name was completely out of the question. It wasn't merely a matter of poor manners. It just wasn't done, period.

"Wha—?!"

Llenn spun around so fast it made a whipping sound. Fuka-ziroh, Pitohui, and M were clearly shocked, too. They stared at the man who had just arrived.

He was alone. Described as simply as possible, he was tall, handsome, and skinny. Over six feet? Because *GGO* was an American-made game, the average height for characters was on the taller side, but this guy had to be at the maximum player height. He was taller than M.

But his body type differed from M's in that he wasn't burly and buff. This man was slender, lithe—like a track athlete. He wore an olive combat suit, one of the pieces of starter gear that every new player had when the game began.

And his face, like something out of a painting—it was a CG avatar, so in a sense, it *was* a painting—was very handsome, indeed. The skin tone was somewhere between white and tanned, and his features resembled someone from both Europe and the Middle East.

But handsome was handsome. He looked like a movie star. As he approached, his white teeth glinted in a dazzling smile—whether that was natural or meant to disarm, Llenn didn't know.

"Oh my good gravy, this is very impressive. What a drop-dead hunk," muttered Fukaziroh. As luck would have it, that was a haiku.

"Wh-wh-wha...? Wh-wh-wh-wh—? Wh-wh—wh-wh-wh-who... who...?" Llenn stammered in staccato. Pitohui grimaced, possibly from secondhand embarrassment.

If she had immediately and forcefully denied that her name was Karen, she might have wriggled out of it, but it was too late for that now.

"It's me! Fire Nishiyamada! We met at the party!" the man said, to her utter disbelief. He actually disclosed his own full name, right out in the open.

"Huh? No way. It can't be…," Llenn murmured, once again unable to plead ignorance.

Thinking quickly to prevent others from overhearing any of this information, Pitohui thoughtfully suggested, "If we're getting into specifics, should we find a private room to speak?"

The player who called himself Nishiyamada just smiled, apparently clueless, and said, "Anywhere is fine as long as I can speak with Karen."

"Let's do what I said, then."

They went into one of the pub's private rooms, which the tall and handsome man observed with great interest. "Ooh… They even have facilities like this?"

It was a room out of a Western movie, where people sat around a table playing poker, and once a man was caught cheating, the others pulled out their revolvers and took care of him quickly.

Once the group had seated themselves at the round table, the man claiming to be Nishiyamada was directly across from Llenn.

"Now let's start over. I'm so happy to meet you again, Karen!" he exclaimed, completely oblivious.

"…"

Llenn—or Karen—was silent with shock. She was frozen like a statue. Pitohui had to speak for her instead.

"Not so fast, pal. My name is Pitohui."

"A pleasure to meet you. I am—"

"Yeah, we heard your name. And I've learned something else about you already," Pitohui said, grinning wickedly.

Nishiyamada leaned forward with interest. "Like what?"

"That you're an absolute beginner at VR games. You probably started within the last twenty-four hours, huh?"

"That's right. How could you tell?" he asked. It seemed to be a serious question, eliciting a shrug of Pitohui's shoulders. She asked him, "And what do you want with whom?"

"Oh! That's right, I was here to ask Karen—"

"My name is Llenn! *Llenn!*" she snapped, a little more in control now that they were in a private space. In truth, she wanted to pull the P90 out of storage and pop a few bullets in him, but you couldn't do that here. *If only we were out in the wilderness*, she wished in all sincerity.

"But you're Karen, right?"

"Llenn! You have to call me that, or I won't respond!"

"Oh… I see… So we have to play pretend like that, since this is a game… You poor thing…," Nishiyamada said. He truly seemed to pity her. It wasn't an act, and he wasn't teasing her. He looked absolutely, 100 percent sorry for her.

Come outside with me, you son of a bitch, she thought, veins rising on her face.

"Hey, string bean. You seem to be under a terrible misconception. Let me clear that up," said Fukaziroh, whose entertained smile was now replaced by a fierce glare. Llenn cheered up, imagining her friend was going to put Nishiyamada in his place with a withering statement.

"I'm the *real* Karen."

Llenn never should have gotten her hopes up.

But Nishiyamada's reaction to Fukaziroh was a surprising one. In fact, it was nearly unbelievable.

"Ha-ha-ha, that can't be true. I looked it up."

Huh?

Llenn wasn't the only one stunned; so were Fukaziroh, M, and Pitohui.

But how? she thought.

"But how?" Fukaziroh asked, at the exact same moment.

"I can't tell you that. I have my own means that I wish to keep secret," he said, shamelessly avoiding the question. "But when I learned that you play this game, I decided to come meet you.

I wanted to speak with you directly again. I wasn't sure it was going to work, so I'm glad it did! I'm very pleased."

"About what?" Llenn demanded as brusquely as she could possibly manage.

"You don't mind me saying?" Nishiyamada asked, to her surprise. It seemed a strange question.

You're the one who showed up here to talk to me. Why would you ask, "Should I say it?" at this point? Why are you here, really?

She jutted her chin out defiantly and said, "Go ahead."

"It's about how I want to go out with you and plan on marrying you in the future."

Argh, I should have known!

Llenn anticipated Nishiyamada's answer, but she did not anticipate (or understand) Fukaziroh muttering, "Oh boy... Never mind. I don't got nuttin' to do with this..."

"What?! What's this? Hey, pal! Let's hear some more about this!" Pitohui exclaimed with great excitement.

Oh nooooo! Llenn thought, realizing her mistake. But it was already too late.

"Aaaah! Arrrgh!" she wailed, cradling her tiny head in her hands, but Nishiyamada talked on and on and on.

He spoke at length about himself and what he did—about meeting Karen at an industry party just the other day, how he'd fallen in love with her refusal to judge others based on looks, how she was the kind of woman he wanted to marry, how he'd raised the question of a relationship with Karen's father, how she'd turned down his offer.

And about how, after a full day of thinking it over, he still couldn't give up on her. So he used his secret methods to find out that Karen played *GGO*, purchased a VR game and system for the first time ever, and came in to visit her.

Incidentally, the name of his first-ever video game character was "Fire." He seriously picked his actual name.

"I see… Based on your story, I can sense your fervor. However," Pitohui warned, her voice steely.

Oh? Is she going to tell him off for me? Will she be angry about his breach of online etiquette and privacy? Llenn wondered, another faint ray of hope budding in her heart.

"…That is not enough for me to give you my daughter just yet," Pitohui finished.

The bud of hope withered before it could sprout flowers.

What do you mean, "just yet"?! And since when am I your daughter, Pito?! What is *supposed to be "enough"?!*

Llenn pummeled the table with her fists frantically out of sheer frustration. *Bam, bam, bam, bam, bam, bam, bam, bam!*

Fire Nishiyamada kept his focus on Pitohui, paying no mind to the irritated Llenn. "You said your name was Pitohui? When did Karen become your daughter?"

"That's not important."

Yes, it is! Wait…no, it isn't? Ugh, I don't know anymore…, Llenn thought. She was getting confused.

It was an already awkward situation that had become more awkward, and Pitohui wasn't going to help things by getting personally involved. It was becoming clear that Llenn needed to turn him down herself and put a stop to this mess.

"Excuse me…Fire? I'm—"

"That's right! Let's do this instead!" Pitohui announced loudly, interrupting Llenn and rising from her chair. She turned around and waved her arm theatrically, pointing an accusing finger at Fire.

"It's not good manners to point at people," said the man who had practically cyberstalked Llenn to this point, employing methods that remained a mystery.

Like you're one to talk! Llenn thought.

"I know that. I don't do it in real life. But this is a virtual world. In this game, I play the role of a very rude troublemaker. I have to keep up my act. It's quite taxing, but I do it to preserve the mood."

What a liar. She only pretends to be a pure, innocent girl in real life, Llenn grumbled in her head.

Fire replied, "Well, fine. Since we're in a game, I suppose I can overlook a bit of rudeness."

You're the rudest one here. You're being so rude! You'll pay for this, Llenn thought.

"So what were you suggesting?" Fire asked.

Pitohui sat back down in her chair and told him—with a delighted smile. "This is *GGO*. A game where we hold guns and speak with lead. You must have looked that up when you learned Llenn could be found here, yes?"

"But of course. I learned all kinds of things about full-dive online games, too. There was a terrible tragedy called the *SAO* Incident that took the lives of thousands, and yet there are other devices and other games that many, many people are still playing today. That was quite a shock to me. I don't understand this world."

It seemed that Fire liked to editorialize, even when it wasn't requested.

"Mm-hmm. And now that you have created your own account to get into the game, what do you think of it? Honest opinions only."

"Oh, I think it's quite barbaric. Shooting and killing people with guns in such realistic and vivid ways… I find it honestly frightening."

I won't deny that it's barbaric, I guess. I had that impression at first, too, Llenn thought.

Once again, Fire couldn't help but add to his statement. "So if we start a relationship, I will forbid my future wife, Karen, from playing this or any other VR game, in fact. Human psychology has absolutely no need for a realistic simulation of the act of murder. It can only have ill effects. My opinion is that they should strictly regulate this space, as they did after the *SAO* Incident."

Come outside with me, you son of a bitch, she thought again, nearly blurting it out loud this time. Something that had existed only in her head as a vague possibility was now rapidly coalescing into a firm, determined event.

I think I'm going to have a very easy time disliking him after all. I'll be more than capable of mercilessly rejecting him. Oh, thank goodness.

"Oh my! What a fierce opinion!" said Pitohui, making a show of acting shocked.

Her clarity returning, Llenn considered the situation. *Is Pito using this conversation to dig up his opinions and show them to me? Is she trying to get me to hate him?*

She reconsidered her negative opinion of Pitohui. At the end of the day, when she saw a teammate in need, Pitohui would step up to help out.

"What do you say to this idea, then? You asked her out inside the game, so we'll decide the answer in the game. If you can beat Llenn, then I'm sure she'll fall in love with you."

Llenn abruptly reconsidered her reconsideration.

"Whaaaaaat?" she yelped. This time, she couldn't hold it in. "I don't even like—"

Before she could finish saying "this man," though, Pitohui interrupted. "She doesn't like making up her mind without a competition!"

"I didn't say—"

"A competition, eh? Interesting."

Hang on there, Fire. Aren't you interested in what I have to say?

But Llenn was too annoyed and exhausted to interrupt. She sank back into her chair, sipping a fresh iced tea and listening to Pitohui and Fire's exchange, keeping her pointed commentary to herself.

"Right? You might not realize it from her appearance, but Llenn's actually a serious gambler—she lives for the thrill of competition. Even I'll admit it. She shows respect to a powerful opponent and will faithfully obey the winner if she loses."

That's not true.

"Ooh. Isn't that endearing?"

It's not.

"So this is what I propose. Next Wednesday, we're going to compete in a team battle royale called the fourth Squad Jam."

Oh, right, we were talking about that.

"Hmm. First I've heard of this event."

It is?! You researched everything else about me! You couldn't look up that?!

"So here's what I say, Fire. You put together a team and enter the competition! If you can beat our team, Superbabe Pitohui and Her Merry Henchmen (summer 2026 version), then you will have my tacit approval to have one or two dates or marriages with Llenn!"

Since when was that our team name? Why do I need your permission to go on a date, Pito? And don't talk about "one or two marriages," please.

There were so many things threatening to make her snap, Llenn was getting lightheaded. It was hard to know how serious Pitohui was being about any of this, but knowing her, it was probably all for real. How could she do this?

"Is this true, Karen?"

Aside from the fact that he was still calling her by her real name, Fire seemed to be listening intently to the conversation. So she earnestly answered his question.

"Do you…think you can win? I'm not saying this to brag, but our team is really good."

"Can I take your reply to mean that we have a deal?" asked tall, skinny Fire with a smile.

I'm not going to lose this one, she thought. *I'm going to stick a knife into his head. Inside the game.*

Out loud, she said, "Yes."

"I eagerly await next Wednesday," said Fire as he made to leave the room.

Pitohui told him, "You can watch video replays of each of the previous Squad Jams, so I would recommend doing that. At the very least, you'll get to see Llenn in action."

Fire turned back and said, "I don't need to bother. I don't want to watch murder being committed, even virtual game murder. That's a very respectable opinion that respectable people share." He made it sound like that was the most obvious thing in the world.

"I just have to win on the big day, right? Good-bye," the tall man said, waving as he left.

"You don't want more information on your opponent? Very confident of you. Suit yourself," Pitohui added with a smirk.

Right after Fire proudly marched out of the pub's private room, Llenn's tiny body exploded.

"I—I don't believe this! What was that?! What was that?!"

Roaring, she thrust her arms thrust to the sky at tremendous speed.

"He is a very unique gentleman," Fukaziroh admitted, grinning. She didn't even bother hiding that this was all very entertaining to her. "You two would make a good couple, right?"

"Wha—?! You—! I—! Let me be clear—I am *not* letting him beat me! If I see him in SJ4, I'm murdering him right on the spot!"

"Ooh! What an extremist! Don't say that in real life, though. They'll call the coppers on ya," said Pitohui before she gulped down the last of her virtual beer. She slammed the empty glass on the table. "That's my Llenn."

"For one thing, I'm not yours, Pito! For another, this all escalated because you were telling him nonsense! Geez! This is not my fault!"

As she guzzled down a second glass of iced tea, Llenn fumed

in general, but not at any one person. Pitohui had suggested the idea, of course, but it was Llenn herself who had agreed to it. Apparently, she was easily swept up by peer pressure.

"Well, I don't believe you're going to lose. Not in the least!" Pitohui declared, albeit lazily. She flashed Llenn a big wink.

Fukaziroh added confidently, "He started his account recently, right? What a wuss. I bet you could kill him with a flick to the forehead."

M hadn't said a word the entire time, until now. "I would expect, knowing that he's a resourceful man, that he'll make use of real-money transactions to hire a team of talented players."

"Oh, I already knew that," said Pitohui.

GGO was a game where such things were possible. Pitohui and M had hired some very capable mercenary teammates for SJ2. To this day, neither of them would reveal the identities of those four soldiers. Who could they have been?

"He'll be able to attract people who wouldn't normally give Squad Jam the time of day but *would* fight in the BoB for a hefty price. If that team turns out to be tougher than us—or even if they aren't but happen to get lucky—things could turn out badly."

"You're such a worrywart, M. But you're right—you never know what'll happen in a competition. There's a greater than zero chance we could just get our butts kicked. Or maybe Llenn will die right off the bat. Even if the two of them don't fight, that probably still counts as a loss as far as the bet is concerned."

"What will you do, then?" M asked her in all seriousness. It helped Llenn cool her head a bit.

GGO was an unforgiving game when it came to death. If you took an unlucky hit, you could easily die in one shot, even in Squad Jam. For that matter, what if the head-on fight with SHINC ended much faster than expected? What if she died in that?

That might meet the requirements for Llenn's participation in Squad Jam, but Karen would have to go on a date with Nishiyamada.

With that despicable man! Leading to an eventual marriage!

And then he'd probably tell my dad about it! It might blow my cover on the entire GGO *thing with my family! They might even force me to quit playing!*

"Oh no…"

Worry was starting to eat away at her heart like storm clouds rolling in. But as usual, it was Pitohui who put a stop to it before she got carried away.

"Did anyone record that?"

"Wh…what?"

"Did anyone take a clip of that verbal agreement? From what I saw, Fire didn't seem to know about that item or capability, and he certainly didn't show any signs of using anything."

In *GGO*, there was a camera item that could record the user performing gameplay feats from multiple angles. Most people used it to record themselves doing cool stuff in battle, or dying miserably, so they could play it back whenever they wanted. Essentially, nobody used them in town.

"No," murmured M, shaking his head.

Llenn and Fukaziroh understood what Pitohui was getting at, too. "Heh-heh-heh-heh. Oh, Pitohui… You are a wicked one, indeed…" Fukaziroh leered at her, looking positively sinful.

"That's right! Let's fight against SHINC and all the other rival teams and use whatever attention is left over to deal with Fire. I'll let Llenn murder him in the cruelest, most sadistic manner possible. And on the one-in-a-trillion chance that she dies…"

Pitohui twirled her index finger around, as if the answer was the most obvious choice in the world.

"…then we play dumb—like our lives depend on it!"

CHAPTER 3

SJ4 Begins

SECT.5

CHAPTER 3
SJ4 Begins

And then August 26th arrived.

The fourth Squad Jam, also known as SJ4—the big day was here.

It was a rare weekday event, falling on a Wednesday. It had always been a weekend thing before. Was there some reason for that? The only way to know would be to ask the sponsor.

It was a sunny day in Tokyo. An energetic high-pressure front extended over the island of Honshu from the Pacific, promising a day of heavy, late-summer heat.

None of that had any effect on *GGO*.

As always, the large pub in the capital city of SBC Glocken served as the main gathering place for the event. And as always, there were dozens of players ready to risk their lives, thirty teams' worth in all, and spectators coming together to drink, talk smack, and enjoy the proceedings on the monitors.

Unlike before, this time, there was no impromptu betting pool over how many bullets would be shot in total by the end of the game.

When the early spectators arrived and learned there wouldn't be a total shots prediction game, they grumbled, "What? They got rid of that?"

"There's an automatic ammo refill every thirty minutes, so they probably figured it'll be impossible to guess with that many rounds."

Another man said, "No…that's not it. Remember how anyone who guessed the exact number would win the same number of bullets?"

"Yeah, why?"

"Well, if they can shoot as much as they want, it'll be a ridiculous number, so if someone coincidentally gets it right, they probably won't be able to cover the cost, even with the five-hundred-credit entry fee."

"Stupid cheapskate author…"

The event started earlier than usual, at noon. Teleportation would begin at 11:50, so if all the participating players were not in the bar by then, they would be considered late and would be disqualified from the event. There was no getting in after the deadline.

It was 11:30.

Many had gathered in the building by this point, taking up spots to the sides of the main door and awaiting each new player's entrance.

"Hello to my enthusiastic audience! I am your favorite commentator, Thane, from the squadron ZAT, short for *Zangiri Atama no Tomo*, or 'Close-Cropped Friends'! You already know what I had for breakfast today—oh yeah, baby, that good melon bread with the cream filling!"

In came the man who always wore small cameras as he played, capturing footage of battles from various angles and narrating his experience in silly ways the entire time so he could later splice the footage together and upload videos to the Internet. His name was Thane.

His entire team got wiped out by MMTM in SJ2, and in SJ3, he said something just short of sexual harassment to SHINC before being completely riddled with bullets.

Here he was again today, and he was certain to keep up a running commentary until he died. This time, though, it was starting in the pub.

"Ooh! There he is!"

"Show us another beauty of a death today!"

People often found his videos more entertaining than the official ones, so the audience was delighted to see him. They cheered as though the match was starting already.

His teammates—Benjamin, Casa, Koenig, Frost, and Yamada—entered after him, but unlike Thane, they seemed a little sheepish about the whole thing.

Thane remained at the doorway and said, "All right! Let's see what famous team will be next to enter the building!" as if he were now the MC. It turned out to be ZEMAL. "Whoa! It's the automatic-fire lunatics, the All-Japan Machine-Gun Lovers!"

They were the team that had improved the most from SJ1 to SJ3. They had become quite popular, because their blaze-of-glory style encompassed both their actions and their (often foolish) deaths. Watching them was always entertaining.

Cheers arose from the men in the pub. "Whoo, about time!" "Hyaaaa!" "Get 'em, boys!"

But then the area fell pin-drop silent.

"Huh...?"

And it was no wonder. The five burly men of ZEMAL were carrying something together. It was...a palanquin made of rods and boards. They were carrying it as if this were some kind of traditional Japanese festival.

"Whaaaat? A festival?" Thane said in English, for some reason.

Sitting in the chair atop the palanquin was a woman, a pretty young lady wearing a beanie and a cryptic, old-fashioned smile. It was her, the woman with the RPD light machine gun whom ZEMAL treated like their goddess. Of course, the audience in the pub couldn't possibly know that.

"Open a lane and open your bolts, gentlemen."

"Lower your eyes. You are in the presence of the goddess of machine guns," warned the two men in the lead: Tomtom, who had a bandana around his forehead, and Max, whose avatar was black. Thane and the rest of the pub pulled back without thinking. It seemed important not to mess with them.

It was a divine sight—or more accurately, a sight you didn't really want to get involved with.

In the sudden silence of the pub, ZEMAL and the woman atop their makeshift palanquin moved to a private room and disappeared inside.

"Um, so…what the hell was that?" Thane muttered, forgetting about his commentary. No one could answer the question.

"Was that…an abduction? Have they finally stooped to abducting women?"

"But…she was smiling, right?"

"They must be lying to her! That has to be it!"

"Y-you think we should call the cops? Like, right now?"

"But…what if she's just CG or something?"

"Bro, we're *all* CG."

The pub buzzed with speculation for a while, and though many opinions were raised, no consensus was ever reached.

"Uh, ahem! Let's get it back together now! Here comes one of the favorites to win it all! The Amazons are here!" Thane announced as attention focused on the doorway again.

SHINC walked through.

First was Boss, the pigtailed woman built like a gorilla; then Tohma, the black-haired sniper; Sophie, the dwarf; Rosa, the tough mom; Anna, the pretty blonde in sunglasses; and Tanya, the foxy silver attacker.

Six intimidating women, all dressed in bright, poisonous-looking green, strode into the building.

Thane screamed, "Whoo! It's the chicks who wouldn't let me touch their boobs last time!"

"Do I need to sue you for harassment?" Anna glared through her shades.

"I'm sorry!" Thane said, snapping to attention. "I won't say that anymore, I promise! So now will you shoot me, please?"

"Do I need to sue you for harassment?"

"Wh-why?"

That was enough playing around with Thane. SHINC shot scowls around the pub and then retired to their own private room. They had a strategy session to conduct. Nobody wanted to do that out in the open.

After 11:40, the teams really started filing in through the door.

"Ooh, there are the Ray Gun Boys, abbreviated as RGB, who use only optical guns! Can they improve the reputation of laser pistols? Or do they have no chance? Behind them is the speedy TOMS, including Cole, who was on the betrayers' team in SJ3! How far can they get on speed alone? And right after them is the military cosplay group, the New Soldiers! Their attention to detail is always impressive!" Thane's enthusiastic commentary came rapid-fire.

Meanwhile, T-S entered as well, their faces exposed, not wearing their signature armor. No one realized it was them. No one had any clue.

"Next up is…"

Thane fell abruptly silent. A group had entered that was outside of the norm.

It was composed of all men. Every last one of them wore a mask and sunglasses. Masks weren't entirely new here; the support members Pitohui and M brought for SJ2 had worn them, too. This was different, though.

"Um, how many of them *are* there…?"

"*Ichi, ni, san, shi, cinco, siete, acht, neun,* ten, eleven…" Thane counted, switching languages for no discernible reason. Eventually, he reached a total of eighteen.

Every last one of the eighteen wore a mask of thin green fabric that covered their whole face. They all wore the same single-lens sunglasses.

In *GGO*, sunglasses were nothing more than a fashion accessory for cosmetic purposes. The brightness level of the world could be adjusted by the player regardless of the shades, and the level could adjust automatically if desired. It was similar to screen brightness on a smartphone or tablet.

The masks weren't stifling at all, either. Players could breathe like there was nothing on their faces and push their gunstock to their cheeks without worrying about it slipping.

The eighteen men split neatly into three groups of six, each with a different uniform. Presuming the three teams were labeled A, B, and C…

Team A had serious camo. Very effective, by the look of it—a mixture of fine brown, green, black, and pink spots. It wasn't a real-life camouflage pattern, so this was probably a *GGO*-original pattern created with the clothing customization tool.

Team B was equipped with *GGO*-esque futuristic gear: dark-blue skintight pants and dark-brown jackets with protective armor inside. They seemed mobile, like space soldiers in lightweight gear.

Team C was in tracksuits—yes, the normal sportswear kind— dark-blue fabric with three white lines along the sides.

"What the…? Are they a baseball team looking for a pickup game?" Thane wondered, but no crew wearing masks and sunglasses played sandlot baseball. The closest might have been Team C.

The large group filed silently through the pub and went into a private room, still in an orderly line. Those rooms weren't that large, so eighteen people at once would be very cramped, but this was a video game. The room would expand to fit the number of people inside, no problem. It was very convenient.

One of the men in tracksuits was noticeably taller than the others, but of course, there was no way of knowing who that was.

The men in the pub whispered among themselves.

"Who are those guys…? They came in together, so I assume they're in Squad Jam…"

"I'm guessing all three squads are working together somehow."

"Seems really weird that they're not trying to hide the fact that they're in an alliance at all."

There had been that plan for teams to band together using the flare signals in SJ3, but those people had kept it secret until the game started. It didn't seem to make sense that these guys would put out all the signs saying, "We're three teams hangin' out together!"

It looked strange to MMTM, too, the next team to enter the building. Their burliest member, Summon, muttered, "A coalition? Who gave them permission?"

"Was that supposed to be a rhyme?" asked Kenta, the black-haired one. Summon simply stared at him and shook his head slowly.

Their leader, David, ever the stern one, said, "We'll beat all comers. But...we ought to keep them in mind. They'll be a threat."

The clock on the monitors in the bar said that it was 11:48. Teleportation to the waiting area would begin in just two minutes. The audience began to murmur and stir again.

"Not here yet, right?"

"Not here yet..."

Even Thane whipped up the nervous crowd, announcing excitedly, "The two-time champion has yet to arrive! She had a bye to participate in the final round; what could this mean? Is it possible she could wind up disqualified by not arriving in time?"

Yes, the fighter with the most glorious history of all, who was champion of SJ1, runner-up of SJ2, and champion of SJ3 with the betrayers' team—the little pink shrimp, Llenn—was nowhere to be found. Neither were any of her teammates in LPFM.

When the clock hit 11:49, a woman's voice announced, "One minute until teleportation! Is everyone ready? Do you have your team lineup all together?"

Normally, this announcement would cause the bar to cheer, but it only amplified the uneasy mood in the building now. Llenn and Fukaziroh had come rushing into the bar two minutes before SJ2. They were setting a new record.

"Whoa...you can't be serious..."

"There's no way they'll go out like *this*, right...?"

A silhouette blotted the doorway.

"Ooh! Oh...never mind..."

Thirty seconds before the deadline, two people in tree-patterned camo jackets and all-black combat gear showed up: Shirley and

Clarence. They were in no rush. It was like they were saying, *No problem, we still have thirty seconds.*

Shirley was scowling like always, while Clarence wore her usual enigmatic grin.

"Whoa! It's the green-haired chick with the terrifying exploding sniper rounds and the handsome dude who got into a one-on-one duel with her! Are they a two-man team this time? Is that it? I couldn't see the prelims, so I don't know... Does this mean they made it through with just the two of them? That would be wild! That's crazy!" Thane exclaimed, not realizing that Clarence was female. Meanwhile, the clock was now at 11:49:50.

Ten more seconds. Nine. Eight. Seven.

"Llenn's not showing up!"

Six. Five. Four.

"You're kidding..."

Three. Two. One.

"Oh man..."

At exactly 11:50, the newest arrivals, Shirley and Clarence, and every other participant, including Thane, blinked into a brief afterimage of light and simply vanished.

Naturally, the teams out of sight, like SHINC, MMTM, and ZEMAL, would have done the same from their private rooms.

"No way... My poor Llenn..."

"I know I say this every time, but she's not yours."

Llenn's team did not show up.

*   *   *

Llenn was in the waiting area.

High overhead in the dark, empty space was a countdown reading TIME REMAINING: 09:59, which promptly ticked to 58.

This was the real waiting room before Squad Jam, the place where you could get equipped, go over a bit of strategy, and still have a good amount of time left over.

Next to Llenn was Fukaziroh. "Yeaaah! Let's do it!"

So was Pitohui. "Let's do iiiit!"

And M. "Let's go."

Each was dressed in their basic combat outfit, but they were empty-handed, not yet equipped for battle.

Next to the four of them was Clarence, delighted to be reunited with Llenn for the first time since SJ2. "Here I am! Let's have some fun today!"

Shirley, who said nothing, was there, too, just bobbing her head with a stern expression.

The six of them were Team LPFM this time around.

Llenn bowed slightly to the two newcomers. "Hi...nice to see you."

She'd had a nice conversation with Clarence in SJ2 but had no idea what to say to Shirley, whom she'd killed before. She had no clue what their team dynamic would be, and it felt quite awkward.

Whether out of keen consideration or total obliviousness, Clarence said cheerily, "Llenn! Nice to see you again! I've watched the videos of your exploits! I'm so happy to hang out with you again! In fact, everyone in the bar was sad that the 'little pink shrimp' wasn't there. But here you are! Where were you?"

"In the farthest room back. We showed up more than an hour ahead of time..."

"That's so early! How come?"

"Uh..."

Llenn wasn't really sure how to answer that—the truth was they'd set their meeting time very early as a countermeasure against Fukaziroh's chronic tardiness. And once they'd formalized their *GGO* login and meetup at 10:30, giving her a whole fifty minutes of lee-way, guess who showed up *exactly* on time? Fukaziroh.

So the four of them arrived at the bar at 10:40, well before any of the audience was there, and proceeded to kill time in a private room until the teleportation finally started.

"Well, putting that aside, why don't we warm up with a little strategy prep? Dig out your waxy ears and listen up, folks!" said Pitohui jauntily.

Over an hour was a lot of time to fill, but the four of them hadn't talked strategy at all. They had mostly spent the time bad-mouthing Nishiyamada and engaging in behind-the-scenes talk about Elza's concerts, the mysteries of the cat sticker on Elza's guitar, Fukaziroh's potential future boyfriends, the bottom-up AI incident that shocked society, and so on. It was all girl talk. M had stayed almost entirely silent throughout.

Pitohui extended her palm toward Clarence and Shirley. "These two will be taking part this time…"

Yes. Yes. The perfect team balance, Llenn thought approvingly.

"And M will be handling the tactical planning…"

No complaints there. I'd be scared of Pito doing the planning. Llenn kept her commentary to herself.

"And as the representative to show up on the Satellite Scan—in other words, the team leader—we'll leave it up to our decoy extraordinaire, Llenn…"

Guess that was inevitable, she thought. *I'll probably end up running through a hail of bullets again, but since we have two more support members, I guess it won't really be that bad? In the end, it'll give me a better chance of fighting SHINC.*

Her heart was soaring at the thought of getting a true and proper duel against Boss and the rest. She'd been dreaming of the opportunity to have a battle for the ages, an epic confrontation in which either side could win—a chance to determine supremacy once and for all.

"And Shirley and Clarence, you two are free to rage however you like! Once the match starts, we can even consider you enemies, if you want."

"Huh? What? What do you mean?" stammered Llenn, out loud this time.

"Whoa, whoa, Pito! Aren't they supposed to be the loyal vassals who stand in the line of fire and die to protect us?" added Fukaziroh, also taken aback. Her extra interpretation of the situation seemed a bit on the cruel side.

"What? You kids didn't hear? We only joined your team so we could skip the prelims. Once the match starts, we're instant enemies. And if I get the chance, I'm gonna get Pitohui. Those were the conditions for joining, and Pitohui said yes. Don't blame me for it," said Shirley standoffishly, breaking her silence at last with the tiniest hint of delight.

"Yep, that's right! I'm gonna beat you this time, Llenn!" added Clarence with a smile and a wink.

"Whaaat? That's not…," Llenn whined, dazed.

"Ah, that's too bad. You'll be fodder for my grenades!" taunted Fukaziroh. She jabbed Clarence in the side with her elbow.

"Ooh! That's big talk, little girl!" Clarence jabbed her back.

But while the two of them bickered playfully, Llenn looked up at the dimmed ceiling in despair.

So we're only going to fight with the four of us, after all… That was a fleeting dream…

"All right, let's gear up," M said when five minutes remained.

Each person waved their left hand to call up floating windows only they could see. All it took was the press of the EQUIP ALL button for their equipment to show up at once.

That led to a transformation scene. If this were an animated show about magical girls, this would be what they called a "bank" scene, the kind that's meant to be reused over and over again, for every episode. Only in this case, no one was flying around or rotating or turning naked.

On Llenn's body appeared a little jewellike anti-optical defensive field (technically, just the generator of said field) and pink gun magazine pouches on either side. By their design, the P90's magazines were quite long, which made the pouches to contain them on either hip quite long as well, hanging down like some kind of miniskirt. Llenn quite liked that touch.

On her back was Kni-chan, her black combat knife. Lastly, P-chan, the pink P90, appeared, floating before her face.

"Here's to another good fight!" she said, grabbing it and clutching it to her chest.

Fukaziroh's transformation was the same as usual.

She wore a vest with bulletproof armor plates and pouches for grenades on the outside. Over her shoulders ran the straps of a backpack to hold all of her ammo for firing as long and quickly as possible. A helmet slightly too big for her rested on her head. On her right thigh was a Smith & Wesson M&P 9 mm automatic pistol, which she couldn't hit anything with anyway.

Lastly, she had two MGL-140s, the six-shot grenade launcher— one for each hand. Fukaziroh's experience with *GGO* had grown significantly, but she seemed utterly disinterested in switching to a different weapon.

As for the plasma grenades, which had been such a terror in SJ2, with M's patronage, she'd acquired a full dozen of them, which was more than before. She didn't have them loaded yet, just to make sure she didn't accidentally waste them.

M wasn't going to trade in his M14 EBR anytime soon, either. The sci-fi-aesthetic gun was very comfortable in his large hands. On his back was the bag that contained his phenomenal shield. On his thigh, an HK45 pistol.

Pitohui's body was bristling with weapons.

Her primary, the KTR-09 assault rifle, had a seventy-five-round drum magazine; plus, Springfield XDM .40-caliber pistols sat in holsters on both legs. On her left side, to be extra prepared, was a Remington M870 Breacher shortened shotgun.

And though you couldn't see them from the outside, there was probably a trio of lightswords in the pouch on her back, which she'd used in SJ3. There were also knives attached to the outside of her boots.

In order for her headgear to actually be equipped, Pitohui's long ponytail had to be temporarily undone, then retied.

Clarence's black combat outfit was equipped with a long vertical pouch for holding the same magazines Llenn used, while the Five-Seven pistol she'd use to shoot them was in a holster on her right leg.

Her gun was an AR-57. It attached to a sling, which she passed her head through.

Shirley didn't change much. All that appeared was a ken-nata knife on her belt and her sniper rifle, the R93 Tactical 2. She liked to use ponchos for effective camouflage when needed, so this was all she wanted for now.

Lastly, everyone summoned the items they were issued by the event. Those would be the Satellite Scanner, which told them their location, and three emergency med kits. Each player placed them where they were most convenient.

In less than a minute, the entire group was at complete combat readiness. Fukaziroh looked at Shirley and Llenn and said, "Huh? What about your pistols? They're a must for this one, right?"

The two answers that came back were not the same.

Shirley said, "In my inventory. It'll only get in the way when moving or sniping. I'll take it out when I need it."

"Oh, okay. Don't know why I was worried."

Llenn said, "I don't need it. I wouldn't be able to hit anyone anyway. I'd rather rush around and use my knife."

"Oh, okay. Now I'm worried!" said Fukaziroh. "C'mon, didn't you read the message? It said pistols are mandatory on this field trip. I've had mine this whole time!" she exclaimed, declining to point out how bad she was with it.

Pitohui walked over to them. "I had a feeling this would happen! If you really wanted to know more about pistols, you should have come to talk to me, Llenn."

She waved her left hand to bring up her window. With a big wave of her arm, the window appeared before Llenn with a prompt: *Will you accept this item?* YES/NO

"Huh?"

"I bought a midsize handgun that you might be able to use, just in case. Put this in your inventory. If the time comes, pull it out and use it."

"But…"

"Take it. The pistol's your last resort," Fukaziroh urged her. Llenn finally considered it bad form to refuse her friend's generosity and hit the YES button.

The window closed, depositing the item into her virtual inventory. She didn't know how the gun worked but wasn't inclined to examine it, and Pitohui said nothing further about it.

Cha-chik!

Metallic sounds rang out in the waiting area as each player loaded their respective guns. It was in this moment that what had previously been awkwardly shaped paperweights of metal and plastic transformed into loyal weapons that could attack on command with the press of a fingertip.

Llenn's P90 had fangs of its own. She never put the safety on.

A little over a minute remained once all the preparations were complete at last.

Pitohui always liked doing something extra at the end, so she gathered everyone aside from Clarence and Shirley into a little circle. Once they were all facing one another, she called out, "All right, gang! Let's kick some ass!"

"Yeah!" the other three replied, because they were nice and considerate.

Shirley stayed silent. Clarence, despite soon being their enemy, joined in with a raised fist of her own from outside the circle. "Yeah!"

"We have just one goal today: to win it all! Also, to win it all! And if that fails, we'll win it all!"

"That's not one goal, Pito. That's three!" refuted Fukaziroh, playing along.

"You're free to do whatever you want in the virtual world! Every face you see through your sights, imagine someone you hate, smiling! It's time to take out all of our daily frustrations!"

Yeah!

"Yeah!" cheered the three others, plus Clarence.

Shirley was also clenching a fist without making any noise, but nobody noticed her doing it.

The person she hated continued her speech.

"But don't get sloppy! Stay vigilant to the very end! There are special rules this time, too, but remember it's coming from that stupid-ass writer! It's got to be something horribly nasty! Don't let him win!"

Yeah!

"Let's do this!"

Yeah!

The floating countdown reached zero.

The fourth Squad Jam was beginning.

✳   ✳   ✳

Llenn opened her eyes and saw a forest.

However, it wasn't a very thick one. The trees were on the shorter side—around thirty feet tall—and they weren't densely packed. There was no grass underfoot. The soil was dry, so it had all withered away, presumably.

The vegetation was what you'd find in the United States, but it bore a resemblance to some wood groves in Japan. The season was winter.

"Watch the area," said M. Llenn dropped into a crouch and swiveled around to examine her surroundings.

The terrain was flat, and nothing particularly stood out to her. The tree trunks were blocking enough of their line of sight to make it difficult to see what might be beyond them. Nothing big, nothing notable.

When she looked up, beyond the dull green of the leaves, she took in *GGO*'s signature red sky, like a sunset even when it was noontime and sunny.

There wasn't a cloud overhead from what she could see. The weather was uncharacteristically nice for today's Squad Jam.

In-game time was linked to real time, so the sun was visible in the sky, directly to the south. The slant of its rays created complex patterns of light and shadow with the trunks and branches of the trees.

There wouldn't be a single enemy team within two-thirds of a mile by design, and with the terrible visibility of the forest, there was no need to be concerned about ultra-long-distance sniping here.

M arrived at the same conclusion. "Okay, I'll check the map. Gather up," he said.

She could hear his voice through the air, but even if he were farther away, it would come in clearly thanks to the comm item the entire team used to talk remotely.

Llenn stood up and looked at her teammates, careful to swing the muzzle of her P90 along the ground so she didn't accidentally point it at them.

Fukaziroh, Pitohui, and M huddled up with her, but Shirley announced, "I'm going to do as I please now. The next time we meet, one of us will be dead. I'm not reacting to the comm at all."

Llenn glanced her way and saw that both she and Clarence had put on green camo ponchos designed to blend in with the forest. They worked quickly.

"C'mon, you can at least check the map before you go. It's not going to inconvenience you," suggested Pitohui as casually as if she was cajoling them to have a cup of tea before they left.

"...Fine," Shirley said reluctantly.

The most important thing to do once Squad Jam started was learn what kind of place the battlefield was and where you were in it. Also, to decide where you should go next or if you should shelter in place for the moment.

The ten minutes leading up to the first Satellite Scan were the perfect time to plan strategy. Even Shirley, who wanted to go off on her own and ultimately defeat Pitohui, decided it was better to stick around with her hated nemesis and hatch her plan first.

M set up his device to display the map on the ground near his feet. Squad Jam always took place on a unique square map measuring exactly ten kilometers to a side, or a bit over six miles. That scale was based on the size used in the individual battle royale: the BoB, or the Bullet of Bullets.

In realistic terms, a hundred square kilometers was quite

expansive. In comparison, the Yamanote Line, which surrounded the center of Tokyo in a circle, encompassed an area of about sixty-three square kilometers. The map was larger than that.

But because a player's avatar never felt fatigue, it wasn't *too* big to handle. Every character could move at a marathon runner's pace, and if you were agility-centric like Llenn, it was more like a sprinter's pace.

The map was littered with rideable vehicles, and often the teams that made effective use of them wound up ranking high in the final results—even when it was just bicycles.

Given that the longest-ranging rifles could do damage from over a mile and typical assault rifles at a quarter to a third of a mile, thirty-eight square miles seemed about right as a venue for thirty teams to engage in a free-for-all battle.

"Now let's see what our killing fields are this time," said Pitohui eagerly, as though she were providing voice-over for the preview of the next episode of a TV program.

In SJ1, they'd fought on flat land. In SJ2, terrain surrounded by castle walls, with a mountainous area included. In SJ3, a sinking island growing smaller over time.

As for SJ4…

M operated his terminal to create a three-dimensional representation of the map just off the ground. It was flat terrain, similar to that of SJ1.

There were lines drawn along the edges of the square, meaning there was a physical barrier of some kind there that prevented players from going any farther.

The most notable features were the roads. Based on their thickness, they were probably highways several lanes wide. The highways were absolutely straight and connected in a cross on the map.

In other words, they split the map into four neat and equal portions. It was like a window, or even the kanji for *rice paddy*. You might call them blocks. In the center where they met, there was a large junction with rounded interchanges like a four-leaf clover.

"Oh, that's very simple and easy to remember," said Fukaziroh.

THE 4th SQUAD JAM
FIELD MAP

AREA 1 : Airport

AREA 2 : Town / Mall

AREA 3 : Swampland / River

AREA 4 : Forest

AREA 5 : Ruins

AREA 6 : Lake

AREA 7 : Craters

AREA 8 : Highway

It struck Llenn as being reminiscent of her native Obihiro, as well as nearby Sapporo. Unlike the rest of Japan, Hokkaido's roads had been built before the towns were formed, so the roads were straight, intersecting at right angles and keeping everything simple.

It would ruin the atmosphere to bring up real locations inside the game, though, and since she didn't want Shirley and Clarence to know where she was from, Llenn didn't say this out loud.

"Okay, let's split the map into four and start with the northeast, yeah? What's this?" Pitohui asked, pointing a long, graceful finger to the top right of the display. The map was always presented with north pointing up, so that meant she was indicating the northeast block.

Everyone could tell at once. When you saw multiple long, straight lines running parallel and perpendicular in a flat place, it could only be one thing.

"That's an airport. And a very big one."

Llenn was familiar with her local Obihiro Airport and Tokyo's Haneda Airport. The latter was very large, with four major runways, but based on the map she was staring at, this one seemed even larger and more impressive.

M noted, "That's four runways in the two-and-a-half-mile range. That means a very open and flat area. Take a stroll out there, and you'll get sniped in moments. Gotta be careful."

Pitohui added, "This rectangular thing between the runways would be the terminal building. You can see the control tower here, too. That would be a very convenient location to control; you'd have a view of the entire area."

The others nodded. Shirley secretly smirked to herself. This was a useful tidbit.

Fukaziroh read the sniper's mind, however. "Yeah, but we're not there right now, O Great Shirley."

"Ugh…"

Clarence pointed at the block below that, the southeast area. "We're down here, right?"

On the farthest right bottom corner of the map was a shining white point. When there was an indicator right after the start of the game despite the lack of a satellite passing overhead, that signaled the player's location.

It seemed the unspoken understanding that the four seeded teams had to be placed in each of the four corners was still the going rule. The rule book claimed that "all teams are placed in perfectly random locations," but nobody actually believed that.

That would mean they could expect a long and arduous journey before they ran into SHINC, but Llenn was already expecting that.

It simply meant she had to beat anyone who stood in her way.

The features of the southeast block were split neatly into three sections.

The farthest to the outside was forest, where Llenn's team was located. A triangle consuming the bottom-right third of the block was painted in dark green. Once you went northwest for a while, a river ran diagonally, with multiple blue lines running parallel. The ground was pale green around them.

"Those are wetlands, then. Aw, man," groused Clarence.

It was common in *GGO* for the area around rivers to be swampy muck, where your feet regularly sank down to the shin. The worst part was they weren't impassable by any means. If it were completely impossible to deal with them, they could just eliminate crossing the mud from their options, which would be much simpler.

The rivers and swamp covered the middle part of the block on a forty-five degree angle.

"Doesn't this mean…we *have* to cross the river…?" Llenn wondered out loud.

If they wanted to leave the forest, they would have to come this way. Crossing the river and swamp would be very difficult for little things like Llenn and Fukaziroh.

M operated the controls on his device to enlarge the swampy region.

"Yes! Bridges!"

There were bridges crossing the river. Based on their size, they were probably two-lane roads. Llenn was relieved.

But Fukaziroh was outraged. "Only three of them?! And they're all straight!"

As she said, there were only three bridges spread out across the length of the four-mile-plus river. They were located on the north, the middle, and the south. Each was at least two-thirds of a mile apart.

Also, as should be expected of a bridge, they were absolutely straight. You'd be a sitting duck walking on top of one of them. Anyone with a long-range rifle could pick you off.

Based on the number of teams in the event, there was probably at least one other group in this forest, so the first skirmish might occur over access to the bridges. And there would be more foes waiting on the other end.

Struggle and wade through the wetlands and river, or cross the bridge and be an easy target? Whichever option they chose, one thing was clear: This was the worst possible starting location.

"This *had* to be on purpose! That stupid sponsor is messing with us! He's picking on the favorites to win, the bully!" Fukaziroh raged. She was in quite a mood. She even added, "Once we beat everyone to win, shall we go and kick his ass next?"

"That can come later," said Pitohui, checking the watch on her left wrist. About three minutes had passed so far.

The last section of the southeast block, once you crossed the river, was city. The lattice of cross streets became much finer, and small buildings were packed end to end, suggesting a residential area.

Nearly in the center of the map was a truly massive yet oddly shaped building, like a giant rectangle ending in octagons on each corner. In terms of sheer size, it was larger than the airport terminal.

M zoomed in to get a better look at its shape and guessed, "This is probably a shopping mall. The middle part is the main building, and the ones on the corners are the department stores. The empty space around it is the parking lot. It's designed to be easily accessible from the highway."

Ahhhhh, thought the rest of them.

In Hokkaido, where Karen lived, there were lots of large malls with supermarkets as the anchor store. She'd been to such places many times, but based on the scale of the map, this one was far larger than any of them. The entire lot, including the parking area, was well over a mile along each side.

Everything tended to be larger in Hokkaido, but they had nothing on the United States, Llenn concluded.

"Hmmm…" Pitohui focused her stare on something.

There was a small track running between the mall and the airport. It looked like a railway connecting the two locations.

"It's running over the road. A tram, I'd guess," said M.

"I know what that it is. It's the thingy that makes noise when you hit it with a stick," said Fukaziroh. Llenn ignored her.

"What's a tram?"

"They also call them LRT, light-rail transit. It's basically the latest form of streetcar. If we find a car, we might be able to operate it. Let me know if you spot one."

"Okay, got it."

"I knew that. That's what I said—if you hit the car, it makes a sound!"

"Are you serious?"

"Can I ask something…? Do you always treat everything like it's one big joke?" asked Shirley in all seriousness.

"Huh? Oh, sorry," said Llenn. Her apology came on reflex for some reason.

Shirley exhaled. "Fine, whatever. I suppose that even when you're having the stupidest conversations imaginable, the big one or Pitohui are always keeping an eye on the surroundings. Well done."

"You bet! Do you even know how many times we've won?" bragged Fukaziroh, puffing out her little chest. Shirley ignored her.

M returned the map zoom to normal and enlarged a different area this time.

"Now let's look at the lower left, the southwest block…"

It was a region with some very strange markings.

The screen was entirely brown, so it was easy to tell it was just exposed earth, but with many circular marks like octopus suckers arranged at random. There were several hundred of them, perhaps even more. Some of the lines even overlapped.

"What is that?" wondered Clarence. Nobody knew the answer, so they waited for M to reveal it.

"My assumption," he said, avoiding a definite answer, "is that they might be craters. Holes left by some kind of attack. Perhaps they were carpet-bombed?"

"Ah, I see. Yeah, it seems kind of like that." Llenn imagined the surface of the moon. They weren't that dissimilar.

M continued, "That would mean that while the ground is generally flat, the craters will be depressed, and the lip of each crater will rise a bit. It'll be tough to traverse, and you won't be able to see far. Not a good place to get into a fight."

"It's the worst! I'm glad we didn't start there!" exclaimed Fukaziroh, updating her previous definition of the "worst possible starting location."

M said, "There's a straight line crossing it," and pointed to a two-way track bisecting it from the bottom right of the southwest block to the upper left corner of the northwest block—a diagonal line across the entire left side of the map. "This is a train track. If there aren't any obstacles, then like the highway, it will be a convenient travel lane. However..."

"It'll be easy to get shot there," Llenn finished. She was the smallest and fastest target, so her standards were a bit different from M, the largest and slowest. It would be deadly for him.

"And then the map right above it," prompted Fukaziroh, causing everyone to examine the last block in the northwest.

The time was 12:05. Five minutes had passed since the team came to a halt.

The audience in the bar knew that the first ten minutes were a general strategic planning period, so they weren't expecting any flashy action at the beginning. This was the time for them to speculate and chat about who would win, which team to pay the closest attention to for good combat, and what new weapons might make an appearance.

Bing!

When the clock hit 12:05, a loud sound drew all eyes to the message on the screen out of sheer surprise. This was new.

The message started off: *I'll announce the special rules early for those of you watching from the bar! Starting five minutes into the event...*

"Ruins, you think?"

"Yeah, ruins."

"So nobody lives there."

"I mean, I'll shoot 'em if they do."

Llenn and Fukaziroh chattered back and forth about the details on the map.

The northwest block depicted a ruined city, a place with many high-rise buildings, much like the city from SJ1. It seemed that quite a large number of these had toppled over, however. A number of the rectangles on the map were elongated and horizontal.

The train track ran right through their midst, like a road. On the lower right side of the northwest block, a little under half its size, was a white, blank space.

"Whuz dat?" asked Fukaziroh.

"A lake. But it's frozen," answered Pitohui without turning around. She'd been paying more attention to their surroundings than anyone, keeping her KTR-09 level and even with her eyes.

Now that they'd seen the entire map, M started in with his usual strategy announcement segment. "All right. As for our route—"

"Everyone, be on alert!" Pitohui snapped, drowning him out.

These were *GGO* warriors, even when they were relaxed enough to be telling jokes to one another.

"—!" Llenn held up her P90 and crouched down on the spot.

"Mmm!" Fukaziroh grunted, kneeling behind Llenn's left and pointing her cannons to either side.

M closed the map and watched the opposite direction along with Pitohui.

In character as a sniper, Shirley pulled the string holding the R93 Tactical 2's bipod legs together, immediately popping them open, then settled down on the dirt with it. She didn't forget to open the caps on both sides of her scope.

"Oh?" Clarence was the last to react. She flopped down next to Shirley.

After the five of them rustled into position, the forest was suddenly deathly still. A few seconds without movement later, Llenn murmured in a voice too quiet to hear without the comm device, "Wh-what is it, Pito?"

"I sense something approaching," Pitohui replied, just as quietly. Both tension and enjoyment laced her voice.

"Sense," huh…

Llenn was conflicted about that answer. In a full-dive game based on signals to and from the human brain, was it possible to "sense" things like this?

Llenn didn't believe it herself, but Pitohui had been playing since the *SAO* beta test, so there were times when it seemed like she might be capable of such things.

Calm and collected, M initially argued, "The enemy can't have reached us yet, and we can't see anything," before lovingly adding, "But I trust Pito's hunches."

"So stupid…," grunted Shirley, who did not love Pitohui. She stood up and engaged the R93 Tactical 2's safety mechanism. "I'm leaving now. C'mon, Clarence, we're going north."

"What? Isn't it dangerous?"

"Nowhere in Squad Jam isn't dangerous."

"Well, I know that, but…"

Clarence took her time getting up. She was about to take a step forward—but couldn't.

"Huh?"

A hand reaching up out of the ground had a firm grip on her right foot.

CHAPTER 4   SECT.4
The Special Rules Go Into Effect

CHAPTER 4
The Special Rules Go Into Effect

"Huh? Hey, knock it off," Clarence said with a grin as she turned around, assuming it was a teammate's prank. "Huh?"

She then saw that Pitohui, Llenn, Fukaziroh, and M were ten feet away from her and all looking quite shocked about something. Of course, Shirley was in front of her.

"Who is it, then?"

Clarence's eyes drifted down to her own foot…

…and she screamed like a little girl.

"Eeeek!"

It was a large, thick hand, reaching up from the forest floor.

The hand was brown, sturdy, covered in rough scales, and clearly inhuman. For one thing, it was gigantic.

And it had Clarence by the ankle of her boot.

"Aaaaah!" she yelped, stuck to the ground as if she'd been sewn in place.

"A monster!" Pitohui shouted, swinging the KTR-09 to face it.

"No. Stop. Wait. Don't shoot me!" Clarence blurted, shaking her head rapidly. Pitohui promptly decided to hold off—

"Taaa!"

—allowing a small pink girl to leap in from the side instead.

Llenn zoomed over to Clarence, positively sliding, and bounded toward the arm with her combat knife, Kni-chan, at the ready.

Shunk! Llenn cleanly severed the arm.

"Whoa!" Clarence toppled backward, the hand still clinging to her foot. "Aaagh! Gross! Someone pry it off of me!"

Shirley rushed over, despite her shock, and helped remove the appendage from her partner's leg—when the ground split open.

The dirt where Clarence had just been standing, where the hand had sprouted, bulged upward and apart as something emerged.

It was a monster standing about five feet tall. This was a completely new and unfamiliar creature none of them had seen in any area of *GGO*.

The monster was bipedal, but its legs were very short, and its arms were much larger and thicker. Its right arm had been severed, now a stump, and glowed green. Its head was not particularly humanoid—it was pointier at the end—and featured round eyes and ears. A large shell covered its back down to its rear end, brown and mottled and filthy from the dirt and muck, which made it even creepier.

"I guess you'd call this an armadillo-person," Pitohui said, summarizing. Her KTR-09 was pointed at the thing, but she held her fire.

The men in the bar could see the armadillo-person appearing in their midst on the monitor, too.

Other teams in other places had their own different kinds of monsters to contend with, eliciting plenty of shocked reactions from the players.

But moments earlier, at 12:05, the audience had already been given an opportunity to read about the special rules.

I'll announce the special rules early for those of you watching from the bar! Starting five minutes into the event, a bunch of monsters are going to appear on the map. Be careful you don't get killed by them! Now as for the population patterns and rules for the beasts...

"They didn't say anything about monsters!" Clarence fumed, finally free of the creature's grip.

"These are clearly part of the special rules they mentioned," chided Shirley, who tossed the hand aside. It disintegrated into tiny pieces and vanished in midair. The two of them hurriedly stepped back to stay out of Pitohui's line of fire.

"Llenn, can you kill it with the knife? I'd rather not have to shoot it!" said M.

"G-got it!" Llenn understood why Pitohui hadn't fired. Unloading a bunch of bullets would tell any nearby teams where to find them.

She used her left hand to prevent P-chan from swinging in the sling and examined the enemy closely, looking for a weak spot where she could land a killing blow with just the knife in her other hand.

The monster's name and hit point bar weren't visible. From what she could tell, a shell protected its back, so that would be a dangerous place to attack. Even a real-life armadillo's hide was so tough, it could reflect a pistol bullet back at you.

That meant she could aim only for its limbs or belly. Earlier, she'd cut its wrist quite easily, so the monster's skin couldn't be that tough.

How much force could she muster with only her right arm? If the armadillo-person struck her, would the resulting damage be too much? Should she aim for the legs? They were too short and low to hit, though. In that case...

An instant's consideration led Llenn to leap and swing her black knife. When she made full use of her agility, the speed made her weapon appear only as a blur, an afterimage.

Llenn's initial target was its arm, to reduce the monster's offensive power. The armadillo-person's left arm fell off, severed at the joint where it met the torso. Before the limb even hit the ground, her knife had slashed straight across the creature's squat neck.

The two-part swing was so quick, most people might have only seen one motion.

The system determined that she'd inflicted an adequate amount of damage and performed the usual sequence of events that happened when playing *GGO* normally.

Bshak!

There was a sound like a combination of something dry splitting apart and something wet hitting the ground, and the armadillo-person burst into green polygonal pieces, crumbling into nothing.

When playing ordinary *GGO*, this was where she would gain experience points, but nothing of the sort happened in Squad Jam. To Llenn's eyes, nothing else changed.

She checked Clarence's damage in the team readout to her upper left. By glancing into the corner of her vision intentionally, she could see health bars for each of her teammates. They were all green—apparently, the grab hadn't counted as inflicting damage. That was a relief.

"Why are there monsters in Squad Jam?! Oh, wait… That's a special rule, huh…?" Llenn exclaimed, realizing the situation halfway through. Her mind worked faster than Clarence's.

Does that mean that Pitohui had sensed something approaching from underground? She's as much of a monster as ever! she thought.

With her knife in hand, Llenn continued focusing on her surroundings. M and Pitohui already had their guns and attention pointed beneath their feet.

Suddenly, there was a sound like a drum being beaten, a rhythmic *ta-ta-ta-ta-tak*. From some distant place in the forest, very faintly. It came from the west.

Llenn instantly knew exactly what it was. And it wasn't a drum.

"Someone's shooting…a few hundred yards away."

Ta-ta-tak!

The gunfire stopped.

"Must be our forest neighbors. I'm guessing monsters attacked them, too," said Fukaziroh.

Based on the location, it had to be the closest team, located at least two-thirds of a mile away at the start of the game. The monster must not have been that bad, since a brief bit of shooting had taken care of it.

"At least they're being reasonable," noted M.

Pitohui had switched the KTR-09 to her left hand so she could hold a silver tube in her right. That was the Muramasa F9 lightsword. She didn't have the blade deployed yet.

With a sharp expression on her face, she gazed toward their unseen opponents on the other side of the forest. Llenn felt like something was off about her.

Based on the sound of their gunfire, the enemy wasn't nearby. They wouldn't be an imminent threat in any way. Why was Pitohui on edge like this?

More gunfire sounded, answering her question.

Ta-ta-ta-ta-tak! Another burst of automatic fire from the same spot.

Ta-ta-ta-tak! Dun-dun-dun-dun! Ta-ta-ta-dun-dak-dak-dak-daboom-dun-dun-dun-dut-tak-tak-tak-tak! A louder clattering followed it, with some deep drumbeats mixed in.

"What's going on?" Fukaziroh darted to hide behind a nearby tree. Llenn ducked, keeping her eyes on the ground.

M crouched and called to Shirley and Clarence, "Watch the sides and rear."

Shirley could have refused but instead followed his order. She and Clarence watched the north and east—unlikely as it would be for their enemy to be coming from either direction—for enemies, guns at the ready.

Ta-ta-tak! Ta-ta-ta-ta-ta-ta-ta-tak! Dut-dut-dut-tak-tak! Kablam!

The gunfire from the west kept coming. The final booming noise sounded like it came from a hand grenade.

"They're having one hell of a battle," noted Llenn, thinking back on SJ1. At the start of that one, some teams who hadn't thought about consequences launched into battle right in the middle of the woods, going all out from the very start.

But as this was the fourth installment of this event, it was hard to imagine anyone doing that. SHINC had fallen into a battle at the very start of SJ3, but unlike this situation, they had been in a wasteland full of stone towers. They had made a strategic choice based on a strong hunch that they would win.

Ta-ta-ta-ta-tak! Ta-ta-ta-ta-tak!

"Pito, M, something's off. I've been hearing gunshots from the same position this whole time. It's one team. Why are they shooting so much?" she asked, unable to figure it out herself.

"I don't know." M wasn't ashamed to admit his ignorance. "Pito?"

It was 12:07. Pitohui checked to see that they had three minutes until the scan arrived, then answered the question the rest of her team was struggling to solve.

"It was that horrible author who came up with the special rule to have monsters appear, right?"

"Well, yeah...," said Llenn.

"We just saw one. Llenn beat it. Haven't seen any since."

"Uh-huh."

"Don't you find that strange? If you were going to stir things up to make Squad Jam more exciting by adding monsters, wouldn't you do more than that?"

"Huh? Well...I suppose so."

"But even with the ammo-refueling bonus, throwing an endless stream of monsters out so you couldn't end up fighting any other teams would seem to be contrary to the point of a game like Squad Jam, and everyone would hate you for it."

"Sounds accurate."

"You need to balance the presence of monsters according to rules that both the audience and players can accept, or the event will get a bad reputation. So if you're the kind of chickenshit jerk who's sadistic but also afraid of criticism, you'd need to think carefully."

"Mm-hmm."

"I tried imagining myself as a little sadist. What kind of sneaky rule could I hide behind at the end and say, *Look, this is just how it works, so it's not my fault, all right? It's still technically Squad Jam, isn't it?*"

"Seems like you found a new skill, Pito..."

"Thanks. So here's what I think..."

Llenn waited with bated breath. Fukaziroh and the others were completely silent, making it clear they were fully focused on her, even as they watched their perimeter.

"My rules would be this: A monster appears if you stay still. If you beat that monster, you get attacked by more."

"So you're saying...that armadillo-person earlier was...?"

"That's right, Llenn. The first one was a scout. A point man. Recon. My guess is that if you stay in one place, a single scout will appear. Let's say you don't move for five minutes. If you attack it, that sends a warning signal to the area. Resulting in..."

"An attack by a whole horde of monsters..."

Ta-ta-tak, ta-ta-ta-ta-tak! Ta-ta-ta-ta-ta-ta-tak! Boom-boom-boom-boom!

The distant gunshots were almost like screams. A shiver ran down Llenn's spine.

If Pitohui's suspicions were correct, then somewhere a few hundred yards to the west, a swarm of monsters was attacking whichever team had started there. And because they were spending time fighting in the same spot, more and more monsters would appear...

"In other words, it makes any attempt to stake out a position for longer than five minutes impossible...," Shirley spat with disgust. The inability to maintain a long-term position hurt snipers the most.

"Then how come we're safe?" asked Clarence.

"Probably coincidence. We didn't use guns—and *GGO* is the world of guns. I bet shooting summons more of them."

"Hmmm..."

The typical *GGO* player would absolutely have opened fire, it was true. Llenn squeezed the knife in her hand. M had told her to use the knife so nobody heard gunshots—smart thinking on his part.

Thank you, Kni-chan. She slid the knife back into its sheath.

There was another person on the team feeling gratitude toward her own knife.

That was a good piece of advice. If any of them pop up, I'll kill them with my ken-nata.

It was none other than Shirley.

But the audience in the bar already knew all of this.

They'd had the rules laid out for them on screen at 12:05.

I'll announce the special rules early for those of you watching from the bar! Starting five minutes into the event, a bunch of monsters are going to appear on the map. Be careful you don't get killed by them! Now as for the population patterns and rules for the beasts…

If a player remains in the same location for over five minutes, a scout monster will generate.

The aggression and strength of a scout monster starts low, but it will eventually strike. If the player moves quickly, the scout won't give chase.

However, if the player shoots the scout dead, a local alarm will sound, causing monsters to flood the area. The same rules apply to those monsters.

Those are the rules!

In other words, if you don't sit around on your lazy butts and stay on the move, this is an impediment you can easily manage.

Squad Jam is a team battle royale, so do your best and don't worry too much about the monsters.

Now get out there and fight!

It was 12:09:30.

The wristwatches on the arms of Llenn and the others vibrated, warning them that the scan was incoming, but it also meant they would have spent ten minutes in the same location.

"Hey, if we stay here, won't the next scout monster show up soon?" Fukaziroh realized.

"That's probably right. Everyone, prepare to move. Llenn, point. Pito, follow. Fukaziroh and I will go together. Last two are the rear guard. I'll be the one to watch the scan."

There was a series of affirmatives from the group. Shirley scowled, but she'd already given up on leaving their side.

Just before they hit ten minutes, Llenn asked, "Which way are we going?"

Ta-ta-ta-ta-ta-tak! Tak, tak!

M pointed a heavy hand in the direction of the frantic gunfire.

"West. Let's put that poor team out of their misery."

＊　　　＊　　　＊

The team adjacent to Llenn's, farther west in the forest, was ZAT.

"No way! Why? Why?! Why are there monsters in Squad Jam? This can't be happening!" Thane, ever the commentator, screamed into his mic.

As he shouted, he fired wildly with his Type 89 rifle in three-round-burst mode, where each pull of the trigger fired three quick shots. At the same time, he yelled, "I've never seen a Squad Jam like this before! How mysterious!" copying the rhythm of an idol singer in a recent TV commercial for ice cream. It was an oddly confident move, given he was under assault by a wave of monsters.

His companions were desperately fighting in the middle of the forest. Pitohui was entirely correct about what was happening to them.

They'd waited in place right after the competition began, which was normally the safest strategy, only for a monster to come falling out of the trees. When they shot it in a panic, the relief that followed was fleeting.

"Now there are more of them! It's a mystery! Why? Whyyy?!" Thane yammered, too busy talking to actually think of the answer.

They formed a defensive circle in the forest, blasting and

blasting again at the monsters that continued to bubble forth from a three-hundred-and-sixty-degree radius. They burrowed up out of the ground, popped out of tree hollows, and fell from behind the leaves.

The monsters had varied appearances, but all seemed to have designs based on real animals, such as monkeys, armadillos, and cheetahs. There was even one with split colors like a panda.

None of them had ever been seen in *GGO* before, and their weaknesses and strengths were unknown, but Benjamin, who used an A4 fixed-stock model of HK MP5, the most popular submachine gun in *GGO*, shouted, "Shoot them, Thane! They're weak once they get close!"

Sure enough, even three easy shots to the torso from the 9 mm Parabellum pistol was sufficient to easily dispatch the creatures.

It took more rounds to defeat an enemy that was farther away, so it seemed safe to say that damage falloff increased with greater distance (and vice versa) and was more extreme with these monsters than in ordinary play against other players and the game's standard enemies.

ZAT shot and shot and shot some more at their foes. They kept the monsters thoroughly at bay, never letting them approach closer than thirty feet.

"It's good to have everyone here fighting! Oh, right! There's that special rule this time that we get max refills at thirty minutes! Got nothin' to lose, then!" Thane announced, shifting the Type 89's select switch from "3" to "Re."

The rifle was made for the Japan Self-Defense Force, so naturally, the indicators on the switch were in Japanese. The "A" setting was for *Anzen*, or safety on. "Ta" was for *Tansha*, or single fire, one bullet for each pull. And "Re" was short for *Rensha*, or consecutive fire. People liked to say that the combination of *A-Ta-Re* was intentionally chosen because it sounded like "hit the target."

He opened the bipod, with which every SDF gun came equipped, and set it down on the forest floor.

"Prone firing position for stability! Forty-three percent increased accuracy according to company tests! Individual results may vary! All models depicted are eighteen years or older!" Thane chattered as if he were reading aloud the fine print in a commercial. He began spraying bullets with the Type 89's full auto mode.

His 5.56 mm bullets hit a monster resembling a freakish mix between a horse and sheep, which was sticking its head out from behind a tree. It soon burst into polygonal shards.

As Thane switched out for a new thirty-round magazine, he said, "I've been thinking, do you suppose those monster designs were rejected models for *GGO* that they're reusing here? I can't imagine they're spending enough money on this to develop completely new designs."

That was accurate, in fact. These half-baked, uninspiring monster designs were all rejected entries from a design competition during the planning stages of *GGO*.

The time was now 12:12.

ZAT sprayed bullets for seven minutes without worrying about ammo whatsoever. They didn't budge an inch during that time, but the game's rules didn't seem sadistic enough that it would send even more scout monsters for not moving.

Eventually, new foes stopped appearing. After half a minute or so, Thane stood up and pumped his arms into the air. "Looks like they're not coming after us anymore! We did it! We survived the special rules of Squad Jam! What a brilliant moment! What glory! This is where we really start to shine!"

In one hand was the Type 89 rifle, smoke rising from its overheated barrel. "Yesss! You held out, partner! When this is all over, I'm gonna oil and polish you and take you to bed with me!"

It sounded perverted at first, but there were more than a few *GGO* players who did things like this. Some people literally rented beds in the virtual space and went to sleep within the game while holding their guns.

Their trial behind them, the members of ZAT loosened up,

pulled more ammunition out of their virtual storage to refill their stock, and got busy switching out magazines.

But weren't they forgetting something?

"Fire."

"Shit."

Shirley swore, but she did as M ordered and pulled the trigger.

The high-spec R93 Tactical 2 sniper rifle was the first weapon fired by Team LPFM.

It unleashed a 7.62 mm bullet equipped with explosives and a detonator that sped between trees and crossed a distance of a quarter mile in 0.6 seconds.

"Oh, my sweet baby, my beautiful darling, how I love you," Thane said, kissing the stock of his Type 89 as the bullet hit his torso.

It exploded there, separating him into Part A, his upper half, and Part B, his lower half, ensuring that he would be doing the rest of his commentating from the waiting area and the common-area pub.

"Go."

"Got it!"

Llenn took off running.

She'd been sneaking closer up to that point, until she was only two hundred yards to ZAT's position in the forest. Then she ran at top speed, in such a way that she didn't crash into any trees.

M backed her up with some sharp M14 EBR fire. The first shot split Casa's head; he was too slow to hit the dirt. The second struck Koenig in the face as he dived for cover. He lost half his hit points.

"Sniper! Enemy fire! Real enemies this time!" screamed Yamada from where he lay behind a tree.

"Dammit! The scan already passed!" Frost swore, realizing their huge mistake.

While M's quick and steady shooting kept them pinned in place, Llenn was setting a new world record for forest sprinting.

"Sorry!" she blurted out as she plunged into their midst without slowing.

An opponent lying flat on the ground is nothing but target practice. Llenn zipped around the cramped quarters, letting loose.

Pa-pa-pap!

"Glergh!"

Pa-pa-pap!

"Aaaagh!"

Shunk.

"Not the knife!"

She shot two of them dead, and as Koenig was in the middle of administering an emergency med kit, she sliced his neck and his hand next to it.

Benjamin succeeded in getting away because he abandoned the rest of his team at the first sign of danger—until he ran right into Pitohui, who'd circled around the other side.

"Hiii!"

"H...hi...," he repeated, just before a photon sword sent his head and body in separate directions.

12:13.

Now that ZAT was lying around them with floating tags reading DEAD hovering overhead, Llenn's team finally had a chance to hold a strategy meeting.

The entire group formed a circle several yards in diameter, their backs to one another. They spoke without being face-to-face. This was to avoid being ripe targets for a single grenade blast.

First, M reported, "What I saw on the first scan was SHINC in the northeast at the airport, MMTM in the northwest, and ZEMAL in the southwest."

Good! I can see them if we go to the airport! I can fight them!

In her heart, Llenn pumped her fist. At least SHINC wasn't in the northwest corner, which would be the absolute opposite side of the map. Of course, their teams wouldn't be dueling anytime soon. They needed to survive until then.

Speaking of which, where did Fire's team go? she wondered. But of course, she didn't even know their team name, so it was impossible to be sure. Over half the teams in SJ4 were unfamiliar, so she couldn't even begin to guess.

I hope he's already dead somewhere, she thought.

M continued, "There were three teams in the forest. One of them is gone, right here. The other team, which is a new one, was close to the farthest southern bridge. They must have decided it was worth the risk to rush to the bridge when they first got a glimpse of the map."

Ahhh, Llenn reflected internally. Their own team was in the very corner of the map, so they couldn't have gotten that far in ten minutes. Llenn might have made it, but slow-footed M wouldn't be able to keep up.

However, if they had been placed within a mile or so of a bridge, they might have assumed a little risk or hedged a bet that no enemy teams would be on the move in the first ten minutes and rushed ahead.

Pitohui said, "That team will be doing their best to cross the bridge right now. Maybe they've already made it. If they were on the move, they probably haven't fought any monsters."

"So does that mean we're the only ones in the forest now?" Fukaziroh asked.

M nodded. "Based on the features of the map, I can't imagine any teams are looking to rush over here."

Of course not, Llenn agreed. Only the most eccentric of teams would actually want to go somewhere as difficult to enter and leave as this. She wanted out of here, herself.

M continued, "I didn't get a chance to say this because of the monster attack, but this is what I was thinking before the scan came in: We should move south or east to proceed along an edge of the map, and then we should cross a bridge or go directly to the wetlands. Afterward, Shirley and Clarence will be free to do as they please."

Wasting no time, Shirley promptly said, "No objections here. Shall we go already?"

Clarence was a bit calmer. "Hey, take it easy. M's not done talking. And I'm sure I know what he was about to say next. 'But there's nothing wrong with staying here'!"

"That's right," M agreed.

Llenn thought she understood what they meant. If they were the only ones in the forest area now, they had the option of simply not leaving for the moment. If they kept on the move, they could both prevent monster attacks and avoid encountering enemy squads. As time passed, more and more opponents would drop out until it was perfectly safe to cross the river. That was a valid strategy.

If some enemy came looking for a fight them or wanted to claim their hiding space for themselves, LPFM could be sneaky and ambush them somewhere along the bridge or wait until they reached the forest, then strike with full force.

"Hmm. It's not a bad strategy, but that will mean that me, Rightony, and Leftania won't get a chance to shine. Oops, forget about me. What I mean is, Pito won't get a chance to rage. Or Llenn, and so on, and so on," said Fukaziroh, hastily covering her true opinion.

"It's not a bad plan," Pitohui agreed. "If we're aiming to win, I endorse it."

"But you're not?" Shirley asked, surprised.

"Of course we are! But the thing is, more important—"

"More important than that?"

"I want to make sure Llenn gets a rematch with SHINC, so I vote that we go north. Not that it's up to a vote."

Pito... Llenn found herself softening at this unexpected gesture. Then she paused and tensed. *Wait, is she plotting something?*

"Pito, are you plotting something?" pried Fukaziroh, reading her friend's mind.

"Oh, no. No. I've never plotted anything in my life."

"That's amazing!"

At 12:17, M stood up. "Monsters are going to show up in one minute. I'm making the decision for us," he said. "Llenn. Run south."

*   *   *

12:20.

The players still alive in the game all watched for the second scan.

By this point, they'd figured out the general rules: Monsters show up one at a time if you stay in the same place for five minutes. If you kill it with a gun, it summons a great horde for a while, so the best option is to ignore it and keep moving.

This obstacle could be avoided by not staying in any one place for more than four minutes, a guideline all teams were now following. The ones that wanted to lie in wait to set up ambushes fumed:

"That stupid damn sponsor just had to do this to us!"

"Get out here so we can shoot you!"

However, that was something they learned because they'd survived. Seven unfortunate squads had been wiped out either by monsters surrounding them or by other teams ambushing them during a monster attack, like ZAT. That was a major factor in the early departures.

Adding in those who had bounced out due to normal combat, this left twenty-one surviving squads at the twenty-minute mark.

The results of the scan told twenty of those teams something: The leading contender to win, LPFM, was located as far to the right side of the map as possible. They'd been a bit above and to the left ten minutes ago—meaning they'd moved northwest—but had now pulled back as far as they could.

Many of those players assumed, *They've chosen to hide out in the woods, then.* They mocked the lack of fighting spirit reflected in such a strategy.

The players on a few teams who knew Llenn better than that, though, realized, *Oh, this is a trap. You can't rely on the locational information at this point in the game at all.*

"There's no way Llenn's team is gonna castle up. You people are idiots." One of the watchers in the pub snorted at those who mocked the team for choosing to "hide."

"What'd you call me?!"

A fight nearly broke out. The man's reference to "castle" came from the chess strategy of sealing the king behind other pieces for defensive purposes. Fighting in a bar was like something out of an American movie, but there was no way to inflict damage while in the city of SBC Glocken. It just meant they'd be pounding one another with no effect whatsoever, so they gave up and settled on nasty comments instead.

"Hey, Mr. I'm-So-Much-Smarter-Than-Everyone-Else, maybe you could share the gift of your immense knowledge with us idiots. We couldn't help but notice that little light shining in the very corner of the map."

The first man snorted again and said, "That little pink one can run three miles in ten minutes if she wants to. She could get to the bridge before the next scan. It's a trap they're setting up by leaving their leader in that spot."

Llenn stood all by her lonesome.

Three minutes earlier, M had told her to hurry to the edge of the map, so she'd sprinted through the forest and found herself here.

In the southeast corner of the game arena, the boundary that prevented players from going any farther was a barbed wire fence. Metal constructs as thick as telephone poles were embedded into the ground at short intervals, holding up thick snarls of barbed wire with huge points, up to a height of thirty feet. There was more forest beyond that point, but Llenn wasn't going to try trekking any farther.

She *was* curious why there would be barbed wire here, though. By using her time before the scan to investigate, she found that a number of signs had fallen to the ground, presumably from a position stuck to the outside of the fence. They were rusted and dirty but still legible and written in English.

BIOHAZARD! HEAVY CONTAMINATION AREA! ENTER AT RISK TO YOUR OWN LIFE! —CDC

IF YOU ENTER, YOU WILL NOT BE GRANTED EXIT! YOU WILL BE SHOT WITHOUT WARNING! —USDOD

YOUR FAMILY INSIDE THIS BORDER IS NO LONGER YOUR FAMILY. THEY DO NOT REMEMBER YOU. FORGET ABOUT THEM.

The messages were quite menacing.

Ugh, so this is some off-limits area after an incident of some kind? And we have to fight here?! Llenn griped. It was only a VR game, but she had a very bad feeling about this. She hadn't felt alone or scared moments ago, but now she was keenly aware of her solitude. Without realizing it, she clutched P-chan tighter.

Then it was time for the scan. She waited in place, not pulling out her Satellite Scan terminal.

"All right. Wait there until it's done," M told her through the comm.

Okay. Get ready to run again, she told herself, preparing for action. She placed the P90 and magazine pouch in her inventory, leaving just the knife at her waist, her lightest and most mobile state. A few dozen seconds passed.

"Scan's over. Do as we planned."

"Roger that!"

Llenn's boots rocketed her forward along the forest floor.

She ran and ran, directly north through the trees.

Normally, it would be difficult to maintain a steady direction in the woods, but this time, she could cheat. She was simply running alongside the eastern barrier of the play area.

M and the rest of the team were supposedly at the northern edge of the forest area, rushing toward the bridge in a much shorter trip. M was skilled at navigation, so he would be fine, but she was much more worried about Fukaziroh.

The team was supposed to meet up there, then proceed to the airport after the 12:30 scan.

Earlier, M had said, "We'll head for the northern bridge, but we'll wait until we get to the location to decide whether to risk using it or to try crossing the water and swamp instead." He then clarified, "There might be highly mobile vehicles hidden around there. This seems to be an especially disadvantageous part of the map, so we can hope there might be a convenient measure like that to balance it out."

That made sense to the group. Crossing the river and swamp would be easy with a hovercraft or propeller boat, and if they found a car, they could cross the bridge in a blink. In an event where you had to walk everywhere, the effect of a high-speed vehicle capable of going up to sixty miles an hour was huge. Llenn had experienced that for herself.

In SJ1, MMTM's hovercrafts and SHINC's truck had been a major headache.

In SJ2, MMTM had found those damned Humvees, and T-S had the bicycles.

In SJ3, they'd found their own truck, which made life easier.

So they knew they were heading for the northern end of the forest, but first came the strategic choice of sending Llenn away to place the leader's dot in a different location on the map. That left the rest of them free to move in secret, allowing them to search for vehicles.

Of course, setting up a misleading leader's mark was a common trick in Squad Jam. Some of their opponents wouldn't be fooled by this, but M was thorough and cautious. He wanted every possible defense.

Shirley didn't object to the plan, either because she didn't have a better one or because she was going north anyway—or maybe it was both. "That's fine. We'll go with you until we cross the water to solid ground. And after *that*, we're going to split off," she grumbled, scowling.

At any rate, the river and swamp are too dangerous to deal with. Much safer than crossing with just two people, Llenn thought as she ran. *Despite her temper, Shirley's a coolheaded player, and she can swallow her pride to survive. Let's hope she winds up having to work with us the whole time.*

She continued running through the trees, heading due north without stopping.

Through her earpiece, she heard M say, "Twenty-one remaining teams as of the second scan. None moved any closer to the forest. The closest group is a new competitor named DOOM. They were in the middle of the residential area. It's not clear if they'll fight us if we try to cross the river, but as long as we're in the forest, I don't see them attempting to pursue us. Prioritize meeting up."

"Got it! I'm praying you find something!" she said, still running.

It feels like all I do in Squad Jam is run, she mused.

12:25.

"Yahoo! We reached the road!" cheered Clarence, who was running point—the lead position tasked with detecting danger. M's group had reached the foot of the northern bridge, where a road emerged from the forest.

Because *GGO* was developed in and based on America, this road was a spacious two-lane street with wide shoulders, paved with concrete rather than asphalt. It was about sixty-five feet across.

Clarence and Pitohui eyed the scene warily, and once they confirmed it was safe, they motioned for their teammates to follow. After that, the group split up to search for transportation.

Pitohui and M ventured out to where the forest met the swampy edges of the river. It was a large area, as the river split into scattered tributaries. They could see a bridge with low railings extending straight into the distance.

The swampy stretch was packed with reedy grass that swayed in the wind. The river itself was placid and still, reflecting the sky like a mirror.

Thick supports held up the large bridge. The whole thing looked sturdy. This was a design that actually existed in reality, so it had probably been modeled after a bridge from an area that experienced plenty of flooding. The railings were made of chalky-white metal pipes, rising to about waist height. The bridge itself was around thirty feet above the water.

Despite a careful examination, they didn't find anything like a boat that could ferry them across the water.

"It's getting cloudy."

"Yeah."

By leaving the forest, they discovered some clouds in the sky that hadn't been there when the event started. The red sky was steadily turning gray, patch by patch.

"I found it! I found it, everyone!"

At 12:28, three minutes after their desperate search started, Fukaziroh struck gold in the forest on the other side of the road. They rushed to join her.

"Ooh! Amazing! This is awesome!" roared Clarence.

They had a means of transportation. On a branching path, hidden in the greenery of the forest, was a trailer truck covered by an enormous tarp.

It was a vehicle for cargo shipping, with a "tractor," the front car containing the driver's cab and engine, and a "trailer," the cargo container the tractor pulled behind it. It was American-sized, meaning it was much larger than its Japanese equivalents. It felt like standing next to a train car. There were six huge tires along the sides.

They worked together to remove the tarp, which was the size of a huge theater curtain, revealing the trailer's cargo.

The bed was flat, a thick steel slab resting atop the vehicle's frame, with large metal enclosures, called fences, arranged along the edges. Resting on their sides inside were dozens of thick, supporting metal beams about sixty feet tall, like telephone poles. If she'd been there, Llenn would have recognized them as the supports for the fence along the barrier.

They were piled up on top of one another, then tied down over the sides with wire rope. From road surface to tip, the cargo pile rose to a height of thirteen feet.

"You think we can use these for something?" Clarence wondered.

"Swing them around and pulverize the enemy," Fukaziroh responded.

Clarence shrugged. "So I guess they're nothing more than useless luggage… We'd go faster if we dumped them, right? Can we do that?"

"I doubt it," said M. "We can cut the wire, but we can't tip the trailer over to roll them out."

He placed on the ground the backpack containing his shield and climbed up to the driver's seat on the left side of the cab. Given his size, trying to get him and the gigantic backpack in at the same time would be impossible.

M checked to see if someone had booby-trapped the truck, carefully opening the door and sliding into the cab. He turned the key still in the engine, and the truck flared to life with a sound like a monster roaring. Black smoke began pouring from the two exhaust pipes jutting toward the sky.

This was a future Earth, but there was a key-ignition diesel engine still running? There was no point in getting up in arms over that. That was just how *GGO* rolled.

"Okay, it's drivable, and there should be enough fuel to get us to the airport."

"Whoo! Give us a ride! Let's go, go, go! I have my license, too, so I can drive you if you need me to. But you look like you want to handle this," jabbered Fukaziroh. She tried slipping into the passenger seat on the right side, but M stopped her.

"Everyone in the bed. Ride at the very end so you can jump off as quickly as possible. Pito, get my bag."

"What? The women have to ride outside?" Fukaziroh grumbled. He had a point, though. The forward-facing cab would be the easiest spot to attack while they were on the road.

"Ohhh wellll, what are ya gonna do? Everyone on board! Let's get outta here! So long to this stuffy forest! Oops, I feel like we're forgetting someone... Must be my mind playing tricks on me..."

"Don't you dare! Wait for me to get on!"

A small pink object hurtled toward the truck. It was Llenn, who had intersected with the road and used it to speed faster through the forest. At Clarence's beckoning, she stepped back into the trees again, pulling her P90 out of her inventory, before she hopped in the truck.

The team was back together again. They'd found the vehicle they wanted, which gave them the means to rush past the gauntlet of the bridge. The team's women piled onto the spot at the foot of the bed where the tips of all the metal poles formed a huge circle.

But then Pitohui asked, "What about the scan, M?" It was already less than thirty seconds until 12:30.

"..."

M thought in silence for several seconds. Should they start driving over the bridge and make good use of the time that other teams might be using watching the scan? Or wait a few dozen seconds (or even just a handful) to delay crossing, depending on what the scan told them?

He chose the more careful option. "I'll watch the scan."

That delay of a few dozen seconds would launch them into a ferocious battle atop the bridge.

CHAPTER 5
Let Me Pass

SECT.5

CHAPTER 5
Let Me Pass

At 12:30, two things happened simultaneously.

One, the Satellite Scan started—of course.

The other was the appearance of a message displayed to each player reading, *Ammo fully restored!* All the bullets, energy, grenades and so on that each player had used thus far were returned to their initial amounts.

LPFM hadn't used much, but being at maximum stock always felt safe. The members who benefited the most from this rule were Shirley, who had her own expensive and rare handmade explosive rounds, and Fukaziroh, who could blast plasma grenades at an astonishing rate.

They both glanced at their Satellite Scanners as they rode in the back of the trailer. The scan started from the northwest, the farthest possible distance from their position. It scrolled down over the map, revealing the locations of teams along the way.

Llenn checked all the dots in the vicinity of the airport, seeing if SHINC was still there.

"Found 'em! Oh, good…"

There were her rivals, below the airport and to the left, close to the very center of the map. They were on top of the runway.

The density of dots was heaviest just northwest of the map's center, around the interchange and the lake. It seemed the fighting had been heavy there, but it was impossible to know the details at this time.

The next problem was figuring out if anyone was going to be near the end of the northern bridge, where they were heading now. The scan was approaching that spot.

The team named DOOM was in the middle of the residential area, having basically stayed in place compared to earlier. Would they be an obstacle when LPFM tried to cross the bridge?

"Shit!" M swore, a rare show of emotion. "We've gotta move! Hold on tight—don't get thrown off!"

The women riding in the back grabbed on to the wires tying down the poles and handles on the trailer bed. The diesel engine roared even louder, and the massive semi began rolling.

It tore through the forest from the path back to the road. Then, axle turning, the front of its cab pointed north. From the back, Llenn asked, "What's wrong, M?"

There had to be a reason he was in such a panic, some explanation she failed to recognize.

It was Pitohui who replied, "Did you see the map? That DOOM team."

"Yeah. They're still in the same place—," she started to say, then looked down again. "Wh—eh?"

She couldn't believe her eyes.

The dot for that team, still active as the scan was in progress, was now moving at an extremely fast clip from the middle of the residential area to the northeast.

In other words, toward the far end of the bridge they were about to cross.

"Why…?" Llenn murmured as they exited the forest.

From the bed of the trailer, they could see the railing of the bridge, the wetlands beyond it, and the glassy surface of the river reflecting the sky. The truck picked up speed as its engine rose in pitch, but it was a massive vehicle hauling tons upon tons of cargo. It could roar all it liked but could only go so fast.

The scan displayed their own location now, but the dot was

traveling slowly enough that unless the map was zoomed in fully, it was hard to tell they were even moving. As indicated by the quickly scrolling indicator, DOOM was going at least three times faster.

"Dammit! Not only did they find a vehicle, they were just waiting to ambush a team crossing the bridge!" griped Fukaziroh, who was riding next to Llenn on the bed.

"That's right," Pitohui added. "They got their wheels and stationed themselves in the middle, where they could hit us no matter which bridge we took. That's why they're rushing toward the north bridge. At this speed, they're going to block us before we can get all the way across."

The bridge itself was a mile and a quarter long. Watching the movement of the dots on the map, they were going to be headed off before they reached the end. The scan completed, and all the indicators vanished.

"Four more teams died in the last ten minutes. All of them in the middle. Looks like it's been a fierce battle," Clarence observed.

"Thank goodness," said M.

"That's very considerate of you to check," Fukaziroh added.

"Oh, shucks, no worries," Clarence said. "Wait, don't I get a thank-you kiss?"

"In your dreams." Fukaziroh jabbed Clarence's cheek with a finger.

"Aaah! Ow!" she yelped, but she seemed to be enjoying it regardless.

The trailer couldn't accelerate further. Apparently, they'd reached the maximum speed dictated by either the mechanical design or the game's programming, which was about fifty miles per hour. They were moving down a wide road in a spacious environment, making their getaway feel even slower.

"Dammit, this was a mistake... I should have gone off on my own," spat Shirley, arching her head around the edge of the truck to look forward.

Clarence reassured her. "Hey, c'mon, you shouldn't abandon your friends. Or friend, in this case. We'll go together."

Pitohui left M's backpack on the trailer bed and nimbly climbed the pile of metal. When she reached the top, she kept her eyes focused ahead. "I'm keeping a lookout."

From the cab, M said, "I'm coming clean. This happened because I made the wrong call. I'm sorry. If we had driven without waiting for the scan, I think we could have made it across the bridge before they reached us."

"Hey, it is what it is. Everybody makes mistakes. You can pay us back for the low, low price of a bowl of ramen. Okay? With all the toppings, okay? And extra noodles, okay?" Fukaziroh insisted.

M continued, "If the enemy comes onto the bridge with some kind of vehicle, I'm going to ram them, so brace for impact. If they stop and wait at the foot of the bridge or in the city, we're going to rush past their line of fire. Get on top of the cargo and lay flat. That should make you more difficult to target."

That didn't ease Llenn's concern. "Hey! Either way, what about you?" If they had a collision, he would be hurt in the driver's seat, and if they stayed behind to shoot, he would be a sitting duck.

His response: "If I die here, pay me back by playing well."

"Got it," Pitohui said.

"You betcha," Fukaziroh fired back.

"Roger," came Clarence's brief reply.

And Shirley said, "I'll do whatever I want, thanks."

Llenn was the only one who protested. "No way!" Even though she realized it would mean delaying a showdown with SHINC, she suggested, "Let's go back, then! To the forest!"

"When did you become such a child of nature, Llenn?" asked Fukaziroh. No one answered.

"We can't do that. There isn't enough space for this giant truck to do a U-turn, and if we try to go in reverse or run back on foot, they'll chase us on their ride. We wouldn't stand a chance."

"Awww…"

"Hmm," murmured Clarence. "In that case, couldn't we turn

the truck sideways to form a barricade so we can fight on the bridge? These metal poles are really tough," she suggested.

"That wouldn't be a bad idea in terms of defense, but it'll prevent us from going anywhere. If another team gets behind us, we'll be wiped out one way or another."

"No good, huh?"

Dammit. Is there no way to avoid M losing a lot of HP or even being killed...?

Llenn gnashed her teeth in frustration as the semitrailer hurtled down the bridge. They'd crossed about halfway by now.

The forest looked hazy as it grew distant behind them.

On the biggest monitor back in the pub, two images were being shown side by side.

One was a rear-facing angle of the semi, with M driving in the front and the women behind—or on top, in Pitohui's case. The wide surroundings made it hard to tell if the vehicle on the bridge was moving at all, the spinning tires and passing guardrail being the only indictors.

The other image was of motorcycles racing down a major street in a residential neighborhood. There were six of them screaming over cracked concrete, with hardly any obstacles impeding their path.

The deep angles of the motorcycles as they leaned around curves spoke to precisely how fast they were going: at least ninety miles per hour. The bikes were dirty and rusted, customized with all kinds of gaudy and inexplicable parts, just the sort of things a biker gang in a mad, post-apocalyptic world would attach to their rides.

They were so customized, in fact, that it was impossible to tell what model they'd originally been, but they were clearly large, probably at least 1,000cc engines.

All the players riding them were men. They wore simple green combat uniforms, with their weapons and gear stowed away for better mobility while riding. Nothing was visible, at least.

"That's DOOM... So they're gonna take a pass at the pink shrimp's team, huh...?" muttered a man in the bar nursing a glass of bourbon with a large round ice cube in it. His avatar was middle-aged, with a black leather jacket, mustache, and ten-gallon hat. He certainly nailed a particular aesthetic.

"You know them?" asked the man with a mohawk sitting next to him, who was from a different team but had been watching the game alongside the first man.

"Yep."

"How?"

"Oh, that's easy. Because my team lost to them in the prelims. They got a crazy way of fighting, I'll tell you that."

"Ooh! What's that?"

"I could tell ya, but it might be more fun to watch. They've been waitin' for a heavyweight team to pass by. If it works out, there might just be an upset in the makin' here."

"..."

On the monitor, the six motorcycles came to a stop.

They were at the outskirts of the neighborhood where two large streets intersected. The wind was blowing harder, rattling a street sign that was halfway falling off. The message on the sign pointed the way.

Straight ahead was the route to the airport. There was a chain-link fence, and far in the distance behind it was the hazy sight of a control tower.

Turning left led to the highway. The traffic light to control the flow of cars onto the ramp was dark and silent.

And turning right went to the bridge. The guardrail was clearly visible nearby next to the road it guarded.

The men seemed to have made their decision. They nodded to one another. With a major spin of their rear tires, they left large black skid marks on the road as they turned. Then they sped up so quickly that their front tires briefly lifted off the ground—toward the bridge.

No sooner had they started than the men waved their hands to call up their windows. Gear began materializing, glowing bits of light that hugged the riders' bodies as they came into being. Within three seconds, the process was complete.

Everyone watching in the bar, aside from the man in the ten-gallon hat, was stunned.

"What the...? What are they...? What is that gear?!"

"I see them! Six motorcycles! Coming this way! Wait, they stopped!" Llenn reported.

After hearing M's plan, she'd climbed atop the cargo to support him in whatever way she could. Pitohui said she could stay back, but Llenn refused to sit still.

She had her trusty monocular pressed to her right eye, trained on the vanishing point of the bridge ahead. With her tool zoomed to its maximum, she was the first to catch a visual of the enemy.

There were six motorcycles stopped at the end. According to the monocular's distance reader, they were fourteen hundred yards away.

"Motorcycles? Good. What gear do they have?" M asked.

Llenn examined the equipment she could see. "They're...wearing some body armor, it looks like. Kind of like T-S, but bulkier. Almost like plate armor."

"...And the guns?" he said, pausing with what sounded like surprise.

"Well...nobody's holding any. It's weird," she reported. She couldn't believe her eyes, either.

"No...guns...?"

M and everybody else on the team had question marks over their heads. Llenn didn't get it. They were coming to fight them head-on. How could they be empty-handed?

M had said "good" about the motorcycles, because it *was* a good thing for them. A gigantic semitrailer would completely obliterate a motorcycle on impact. They weren't running, though, which suggested they had a plan up their sleeves.

M said, "I'm going to stop," and immediately, the trailer began to slow. If he didn't know what the opponent was likely to do, he wasn't going to risk hitting them.

The trailer hurtling over the bridge began easing up.

"Motorcycles move quick, right? So if they avoid us, then turn around and pull out guns, they could shoot us from behind?" Fukaziroh guessed.

"We'd pump them full of lead before they could manage it," Pitohui told her.

"Good point."

With one last screech of the tires, the trailer truck came to a halt in the middle of the bridge.

"Distance at about eleven hundred yards!" Llenn announced.

The two teams faced off. Both were on the bridge. There was nowhere to run.

"If we show our ass, they'll stick it right up the chute," Clarence observed.

"Isn't that sexual harassment?" Fukaziroh wondered out loud.

"Can you get us any closer?" asked Shirley, looking down at the R93 Tactical 2 in her hands. Their current distance was a little too far for a 7.62 mm rifle to aim properly. If she could get two or three hundred yards closer…

But M refused. "Not when we don't know what they're going to do next." Instead, he asked Llenn, "They're still not bringing out any weapons?"

"Nope!" she said. "Doesn't seem like they intend to! They're just watching us! Their armor's creepy, kinda like a blank Noh mask!"

"What does this mean…?" M asked himself. "Is their plan to keep us stuck here on the bridge?"

"Oh! One of them moved! They're racing toward us!"

"And the rest?"

"Just the one! He's really speeding up!"

Next to Llenn, Pitohui steadied her KTR-09 against her shoulder, but her target was still out of range.

"Should I do it? Once it gets closer, I can get a good shot," volunteered Shirley, but M ignored her.

"Everyone off the truck!" he shouted, as loud as he'd ever spoken.

"Huh? Why? What's the—? *Dwaaaa!*" Llenn stammered when Pitohui kicked her to the side. It was a vicious blow.

"Hyaaaa!" She fell from thirteen feet atop the pile of metal to the street. But with her tremendous agility, Llenn was able to recover her balance in the air, landing feetfirst and spinning to diffuse the momentum of the kick.

"Guh!" She came to a stop when her back slammed into the railing at the side of the bridge.

She was worried about hit point loss from a shock that bad, but it turned out to be nothing. Pitohui then jumped off the cargo bed, crouching to soften the impact so she could maintain her grip on her gun.

Back behind the truck, Fukaziroh and Shirley had hit the pavement, followed by Clarence, who'd kicked M's backpack off the edge.

At that very moment, the truck's exhaust piped belched black smoke again as it resumed moving. M was driving it forward… without anyone else on board.

"Huh? W-wait, M!" Llenn shouted, but he didn't respond. When Pitohui approached, Llenn demanded, "What's going on?!"

"This is bad… I just hope it's in time…," the other woman said, her tattooed cheeks twisted into a grimace.

Even Llenn knew something terrible was happening, but she couldn't tell yet what that was, exactly.

*   *   *

M jammed the acceleration pedal to the floor. The trailer's pickup was as slow as a turtle. He could see a bike ahead of him on the bridge, very small—but rapidly getting larger.

Once he'd gotten up to a certain speed, he murmured, "Hope this is in time...," as he gently turned the wheel right, then jammed it left as hard as he could.

What happens when you yank on the wheel of a semitrailer? Something you should never try in real life.

When the cab in the front turned left, the momentum of the trailer behind it, with all those tons of metal piles on the back, continued moving forward. The joint that connected the truck to the trailer shifted, causing the entire vehicle to go into a rapid left rotation. The tires screeched and smoked as the massive body wobbled.

The cab portion, with M inside, broke through the guardrail and off the bridge, though it didn't fall. The cargo trailer was still on the move. It lost balance and began toppling to the right.

"Oh no..." Llenn gasped. As the semitrailer raced off, about two hundred yards away now, it was turning over. "Pito! Look! It's flipping over!"

"Yes, on purpose! He pulled it off! Way to go, M!"

"Huh?"

The truck's tires went airborne. The massive vehicle landed on its side, filling the air with a deafening array of sounds.

Zbwaooo! The engine suddenly roared at a higher pitch, as it no longer needed to roll the tires over the ground.

Grakk! The trailer bed collided with the road, smashing into the heavy concrete.

Gwonggg! The frame of the vehicle vibrated like a bell from the impact.

P-p-p-pchak! The cables holding the cargo in place snapped in rapid succession.

Shlagagagagagarang! The huge pile of metal poles rolled free over the surface of the bridge.

Combined into one orchestral movement, it shook the very world with a clamor rivaling any amount of gunfire.

Zabwagrakwonnngpchkagagagagarabooom!

The entire bridge rumbled beneath their feet. "Whoa. That's gotta be at least a two or three on the scale," Fukaziroh guessed.

On its side, the semi continued sliding forward, the metal scraping up a shower of sparks. From LPFM's vantage, the underside of the vehicle became visible, with all of its wheels, axles, and ladderlike frame parts.

The trailer and all of its scattered metal cargo completely blocked off the road now.

"Hopefully that will be enough of a defense...," Pitohui murmured.

"A-against what?" stammered Llenn.

The video screens in the bar offered the clearest picture of what had happened. They had a diagonal aerial shot overlooking the bridge.

The semitrailer zoomed forward, then turned hard and toppled over sideways, while a single motorcycle rushed toward it with incredible speed from the other side. It didn't budge from its course.

The man riding the bike had on bulky armor that covered his body and head. Unlike the protection T-S wore, this armor left his back completely exposed. It only offered cover for his front.

On the man's back jutted a large pack that closely resembled M's.

While the rest of the audience watched, holding their breath, the man in the ten-gallon hat muttered, "Get 'em."

The bike shot forward like an arrow, and just before it made contact with the metal poles that covered the road—the man riding it exploded.

The first thing Llenn noticed was the rumbling beneath her feet.

"Huh?"

She felt a shock wave—from something happening on the other side of the toppled semitrailer.

"Huhhh?"

Finally, a shock wave knocked her tiny body backward.

"Aieeeeeeee!"

The audience in the pub had the perfect view of the blast.

Orange flames filled the screen, wreathed by a white sphere. The force of the blast changed the density of the air, compressing the water vapor into a momentary piece of natural artistry.

The wave pushed outward to the sides and above as crimson flames and black smoke burst from the center in a sphere like the face of the devil himself.

Then the entire fireball turned into gray smoke that rose toward the sky.

The drink glasses and windows in the bar rattled with the sound of the booming explosion through the monitor speakers.

"Eep!"

"Whoa!"

"Damn!"

A number of people in the crowd tensed in shock. The screen went completely gray—everything was hidden by smoke.

Nearly a minute later, the haze slowly cleared to reveal…the charred surface of the bridge, guardrails missing on either side, a number of twisted metal pipes, the body of the trailer truck pushed a good thirty feet back, and a massive mushroom cloud above it all, climbing and climbing.

It was a mammoth explosion.

A large plasma grenade, nicknamed "the grand grenade," was the greatest single weapon players could wield in *GGO*, and whatever caused this was at least as powerful as those—in fact, it dwarfed their effects.

But in this case, the lack of a pale-white plasma surge made it clear this was a typical combustion explosion.

"What was thaaaaaat?" the audience screamed.

"Exactly what it looked like—an explosion. Though it also came with a shock wave, so I guess technically you'd call it a detonation? I suppose we don't make much of a distinction in Japanese…," answered the man in the ten-gallon hat. When the shocked crowd said nothing, he continued, "You saw that big ol' backpack he had on? It was packed full of high-powered explosives."

"Y-you mean…*that's* how they attack?"

"You bet. DOOM wears armor only on the front. Explosives are on the back. In other words, they're all suicide bombers."

"Ee-eep?"

As soon as Llenn recovered her wits, Fukaziroh's face was right in front of hers.

"Yo, you alive…?"

The pink girl was lying on top of her friend whose body was directed upward, propped up by her large backpack. It practically looked like they were about to kiss. A light veil of smoke filled the air around them.

"Somehow…but my head's all woozy…"

"That was an unbelievable explosion. You got blasted all the way over here like a leaf. If I hadn't stopped you, you'd have gone back to the forest all by yourself."

"Oof. Thank you…"

Llenn slowly lifted herself up for a quick inspection. Fortunately, her P90 was still present in the sling. However, she couldn't find her trusty monocular. That might have been jarred loose from her hand when Pitohui kicked her. In which case, it had probably fallen off the bridge already.

Well, there was no use mourning it now. She checked the state

of her hit points. Being blasted a few dozen yards and hitting Fukaziroh had depleted some, but it was only about five percent.

Then she glanced at the team's totals. All of the women were fine.

"What about M?!"

She expected him to be dead. He'd been closest to the explosion, after all.

To her surprise, though, his HP gauge was all green. He was completely unharmed.

"Whew..." She sighed with relief.

"I'm...all right...," M said through the comm, although his voice sounded weak.

"You jumped down into the swamp from the cab when it was jutting over the side, didn't you?" Pitohui confirmed. "The blast can't push down through feet of concrete." She walked closer. "What's the state of things down there? Can you get back up?"

"Nope... I'm stuck up to my neck...completely trapped in the muck. I'd appreciate you scooping me out after it's done."

"Then wait there for now."

"All right..."

Nearby, Clarence and Shirley were getting back up, each holding their weapon.

"What the heck was that...?"

"An explosion... Shit!"

Then Pitohui warned, "Everyone, back up on the truck right now! The next one's coming!"

"N-next one...?" Llenn asked. She still didn't have a grasp on the situation.

Pitohui turned to her, grinning with delight. "They're suicide bombers! And there are five of them left!"

"When the battle in the preliminary round started, they kept their distance, so we thought somethin' was funny...," said the man in the ten-gallon hat with heavy inflection. He had the audience in the palm of his hand now. "As you know, the battlefield's one long corridor, to ensure you get the battle goin' and over with. It was a rocky canyon with plenty of cover. They didn't attack, so we went after 'em. And then, when we reached the middle of the canyon..."

He closed his eyes. No one could tell if this was an affectation or if he really was reliving the terror and regret of the battle.

"One man. They sent a single man to fight. He appeared out of nowhere from behind a boulder, blockin' our shots with his armor. He chased and chased us, like he was tryin' to grab us. Like a zombie..."

"And then he goes boom...?"

"Yep. Just like that one now. That was all it took to knock our entire team out of the prelims. I looked it up later and discovered the lethal range of an explosion has a radius of about a hundred and fifty feet. If you don't have sturdy cover within that radius, the shock wave is sure to kill ya. Even at two hundred feet, you're in big trouble."

Some of the crowd listening to him went pale.

"So Llenn's team only survived because of how tough the metal and the trailer were..."

"Yikes... What a brutal way to fight..."

"But it was superefficient, wasn't it? You can trade one member's death to kill several of the enemy..."

"There's no way they'll win Squad Jam, though."

"True. Still, if they're able to take out LPFM..."

Four women ran for the semitrailer.

"Suicide attacks! The calling card of scum!" snarled Shirley.

"You shoot people with explosive bullets. You're one to talk!" Clarence retorted, greatly entertained.

"Ahhh, I see. So that's why they sent only one bike to attack us. I'm amazed at how M and Pito can figure these things out so quickly," said Fukaziroh, impressed.

An act that guaranteed one's own death—Llenn wondered if that really counted as an "attack" or if it was more a strategy.

"I guess anything goes in *GGO*," she murmured. "This isn't reality…"

It was a video game world. If that was their strategy, there was no use getting upset over it. More important was surviving this virtual encounter. She wanted to fight SHINC.

In all honesty, this was a very bad situation in which they'd found themselves. If they weren't careful, all of the women on the team could get wiped out, leaving only M alive, and he was unable to move. That would be the opposite of what she'd assumed was going to happen moments earlier.

The four of them reached the toppled semitrailer, Llenn being the first. She climbed about eight feet, using the tires and frame of the vehicle's underside as footholds and handles.

Once her face was over the top, she could see farther down the bridge. The smoke had cleared.

The site of the explosion was completely blackened, resembling a huge ink spill on the ground. There was no trace of the guardrails on the either side of the bridge.

The metal poles that spilled off the truck were completely blocking the road, and a few of them closest to the blast were either twisted up like handblown glass sculptures or broken into pieces.

Thanks to the way the cargo was scattered, the motorcycles couldn't get any closer, forcing the riders to find a different way to deliver their explosives. A few of the poles were still stacked against the body of the truck, acting as extra defense.

M's split-second decision had saved the group from catastrophe.

If he'd run into their opponents or tried to pass without realizing their plan, the entire team might be sitting around in the waiting area at this very moment.

Still, there was no time for relief.

With each explosion that followed, the number of metal poles to absorb the blast would decrease. Eventually, the truck itself might be destroyed. Could they withstand five more of those bombs?

"Here they come!" shouted Shirley, who was watching through her scope.

The other three could see the second motorcycle for themselves. It was just a little speck, at a distance of about five hundred yards.

"Wah-ha-ha-ha! You fools! You rush into the flames of your own death! Taste the scarlet fire that is the embodiment of my wrath! Burn the enemy to a crisp, my 40 mm grenades!" taunted Fukaziroh, as though she were casting some kind of spell.

Pomp-pomp-pomp-pomp-pomp-pomp.

A succession of half a dozen grenades flew about four hundred yards away.

Fukaziroh could shoot her projectiles to any spot. Her timing was perfect. They were exactly primed to go off in succession right as the motorcycle reached that position.

"Oh?"

But when you could see the bullet line, dodging the curve of a lobbed grenade was all too easy. The DOOM member let go of the accelerator and hit the brakes, locking the rear tire and leaving a black line on the road as he came to a stop. The six explosions detonated a safe distance in front of him. When the lighter plume of smoke cleared, he resumed his advance.

"Hey, screw you! Those grenades aren't free!" Fukaziroh fumed for some reason.

"Die…"

Shirley fired her sniper rifle. It was a very quick shot without a bullet line, but the enemy seemed to know it was coming. An easy tilt of the bike caused the projectile to pass through empty space instead.

Rather than riding straight, he switched to a sequence of quick, random wavy curves, making full use of the width of the bridge. It was a simple tactic but effective for dodging snipers.

"Dammit!"

Shirley quickly reloaded, but she didn't fire the second shot.

"What's wrong? Out of bullets?" Fukaziroh asked.

"It's a waste of ammo. They cost a lot."

"C'mon, don't skimp out on the battlefield!"

"Are you a birdbrain?"

Clarence interjected, "Have *both* of you forgotten that we get all our ammo back every thirty minutes?"

When the motorcycle got within three hundred yards, Pitohui let loose with her KTR-09 on fully automatic. "Take this!"

Her lithe, powerful frame absorbed the recoil, sending the empty cartridges spinning into the air to clatter and bounce on the roadway below. The bullets shot faster than the speed of sound.

But even with Pitohui's excellent marksmanship, it wasn't easy to hit a distant target shifting at random, and with her finger held down, the bullet line appeared, making it easier to dodge. Her drum magazine went lower and lower without her landing a shot.

Five seconds and over sixty bullets later, her line of fire finally caught its target, creating a vivid shower of sparks—from both the motorcycle and the rider's body.

The body armor stopped the bullets, but the motorcycle couldn't. The rubber on its front tire tore loose, destroying the wheel. The bike shuddered before toppling over at high speed, ripping the rider from the vehicle.

"Got him!" Llenn cheered, pumping her fist quickly.

The motorcycle smashed against the guardrail, completely wrecking what was already falling apart.

But the rider was fine. He slid along the road, grinding against it with his armor, then stood up and started running the remaining hundred and fifty yards on his own two feet.

"No way!"

The tenacity was astonishing. It was a sacrificial act, one that could be executed only once. The man must have had a considerable agility stat, because he was approaching fast.

"Get away, you perverted weirdo!" Clarence opened fire with her AR-57.

Like Llenn's P90, it shot so fast that there was hardly any room between the sounds. The empties poured out of a hole on the bottom of the gun in the spot where an M16 model would have inserted its magazine.

The bullets were indeed hitting their mark left and right, but all of them were deflected by the bomber's heavy armor. They didn't even slow him down.

Uh-oh, this isn't gonna work. Llenn sensed as much. She didn't fire a single shot of her own. Pitohui started to exchange drum magazines.

Kablam! Shirley's R93 Tactical 2 issued a booming sound directly beside her. The gun's muzzle brake vented its exhaust gas to the sides and onto the people standing in its path. Llenn's hat shook.

She might have trouble hitting a motorcycle off in the distance, but an approaching human target was no problem. The round hit him on the thigh and exploded. It didn't break through the armor but did transfer the force of the shot to him.

He lost his balance and fell over, exposing his back. He was about sixty yards away from the truck—and his targets.

"Get down!" Pitohui ordered. They had to leap back off the truck they'd gone to the trouble of climbing.

They jumped at the exact same moment the fallen sacrifice pulled the cord to set off his explosives.

"Whoa!"

The second blast might not have been as surprising as the first, but it was just as powerful. The world shook, and the sideways trailer was pushed back a little. The scraping of the frame against the concrete was unpleasant even through the roar of the blast. The force of the explosion threw a number of the metal poles into the air, and they fell into the swamp below.

A moment later, smoke filled the area, covering up the already-clouded sky. It was quite a gust. It was like the world had switched to gray fog in a single instant.

"Gaaah! What a public nuisance!" Fukaziroh fumed, surrounded by roaring and smoke.

"But we got through the second one! Maybe they'll think twice about sending more?" Llenn hoped naively.

"Hmm. I would probably send the rest as soon as the smoke clears. If we're having this much trouble with one at a time, there's no way we can handle four," Clarence pointed out wisely.

"..."

It was absolutely true. Llenn had no counterargument.

"Oh well, then. Shall I shoot my special blue friends? Hmmm?" Fukaziroh grinned at Llenn. Of course, she had missed with all her last shots.

"That's it! Maybe your plasma grenades will do the trick!" Llenn felt like she'd just seen sunlight peeking through a mass of storm clouds. Given the wide range of damage her grenades could do, Fukaziroh might be able to cover the whole width of the bridge...

"Fuka, don't. Plasma grenades physically break down everything within their blast range, remember? The bridge is still holding up. You want to destroy the whole thing? Not only will we not be able to cross, it might even cause *our* section to crumble from lack of support."

Argh! It's no good! The sunlight Llenn saw had only been a flash of lightning after all.

"Then what do we do?!"

"So...you think they've won, then?"

People in the audience at the bar were certain LPFM were done for.

The four bikes were waiting while the smoke cleared, but once it had, they could rush up close, ditch the wheels, then charge together as a group...

"If a single one of them can get over the truck before a teammate blows himself up—"

"They can do it! You got this, DOOM!"

"Go on! Get 'em!"

But while the others cheered, one person in the crowd muttered, "You were all rooting for Llenn just a minute ago..."

"Look, I'm here to see some upsets!'"

"That's the thing about being a spectator. You got no loyalty..."

"Hmph! And what about you, huh? Be honest."

"I wanna see it! I wanna see them lose big-time, right here and now!"

"Right?!"

The man in the ten-gallon hat sipped his bourbon and drawled, "I been playin' *GGO* a long time, but I ain't never thought of a strategy like this one... It's the perfect takedown—one that fully understands this is a game. DOOM is the perfect name for a team like that..."

He lifted his glass to the four players on the screen who were straddling their motorcycles, readying themselves for a race to their own deaths, and said, "Your toast..."

But nobody else realized he was making a terrible pun that could be construed as "you're toast."

On top of the bridge in Squad Jam, the members of DOOM sitting on their post-apocalyptic motorcycles shared a final chat before their last ride.

"We can do this! Let's all go in together this time!"

"Okay! We can do it! Man, this is fun!"

"I can't believe we're gonna get the chance to beat the champions!"

"I'm so glad we spent all that time playing motorcycle games! We're so lucky!"

For being covered in armor and strapped with bombs, they were actually quite happy-go-lucky. They seemed young.

No surprise that every member of their team was in ninth grade. They were all friends at a famous private middle school and members of a club there called *Domo! Welcome to the Cyberworld!* If only the man in the bar knew that DOOM was merely an anagram for the word *hi* in Japanese...

It was a feeder school, so the kids could ascend into further education without having to worry about entrance exams. That meant they had time to get heavily into VR games, so they tried out all kinds together under the guise of "studying" them. Incidentally, they were all from rich families.

They'd been converting their characters from game to game as they went and were recent arrivals to *GGO*. They'd heard about the team battle-royale event and wanted to give Squad Jam a shot.

"Let's test ourselves to see how far a newly converted team of rookies can get!" they decided. Since they were converting from other games, their characters' basic stats were pretty high, but they had neither the marksmanship nor knowledge that came with playing *GGO* nor any fancy guns. Even the preliminary round seemed like a major challenge.

But they didn't give up.

They watched Squad Jam footage and thought very hard until they came up with the scheme to blow themselves up with massive bombs. With some help from real-money purchases, they assembled the heavy-duty armor and explosives they would need.

There wasn't a single gun among the entire team.

As the smoke silently cleared, Llenn was panicking.

"What should we do what should we do what should we…?"

"We do what we can. We'll make it count! We're not gonna lose here!" Shirley focused her determination as she approached the truck.

"That's true. We'll blast 'em away again. All these bullets are coming back, one way or another," said Clarence, ever the optimist.

"Should I use my pistol this time?" said Fukaziroh, who was always spirited, at least.

Ugh! Dammit! Don't get upset! thought Llenn, who realized she was mentally weaker than her teammates. She gnashed her teeth with shame.

With what little time they had left, she used her brain. *How do you stop four people on speedy motorcycles before they can blow themselves up?*

"…"

Pitohui watched her thinking.

How do you stop four people on speedy motorcycles, speedy motorcycles, speedy, speedy…speedy…

"Ah!"

Something clicked in her mind.

A plan occurred to her as she considered what items she needed, and luckily, the person who had them was standing right there with the materials in question in her palms.

A silver tube in each hand.

"Ah-ha-ha-ha! You've got it, Pito!"

They were exactly what she wanted. Llenn held out her hands and took the tubes from her teammate.

"I'll be right back!"

"Let's go!"

"Yeah!"

"Uhhh!"

"Charge!"

The four remaining members of DOOM revved their accelerators with their right hands and connected their clutches with their left. Four motorcycles began accelerating all at once.

"Don't stick too close! But don't lag too far!" instructed the one in the lead. The other three followed behind by fifty yards. They spread out in a formation just wide enough that each had a clear view of what was ahead.

The bikes had high-end engines and were going a hundred and ten miles an hour in mere seconds. The game didn't seem to let them go any faster than that.

The enemy was four hundred yards away.

Suddenly, a group of bullet lines rose up from the trailer and fell toward them. Six in total.

"Are those grenades?"

They considered slowing down, but the lines dipped lower. Now they would land only a hundred yards in front of the semitrailer instead. Promptly, the lines started vanishing from the far side.

That meant the grenades had already been fired, erasing the lines as they traveled along their trajectories. What was the point of that attack? There was no way it was going to hit them.

"What was that...?"

"Dunno...," a few of the other boys muttered. They maintained their speed this time.

Once the lead rider was three hundred yards away, the six grenades exploded two hundred yards in front of him, belching black smoke to cover the area.

"Oh! It's a smoke screen!"

"We're all right! It'll clear up soon! Keep going!"

Four motorcycles traveling fifty yards every second and carrying four suicide bombers raced for the smoke—and the enemies waiting behind it.

Two hundred yards to go.

"Hmm?"

As the smoke from the grenades cleared over the road ahead, they saw a small pink figure in the middle of the bridge, racing toward them.

"This road is off-limiiiiiiiiiiiiits!" Llenn screamed, sprinting with all her might.

In the brief window that Fukaziroh's smoke grenades offered cover, she'd leaped over the semitrailer and covered more than a hundred yards.

Just ninety remaining to the motorcycles.

"Whoa! Huh? What the—?"

For the first instant, the rider in the lead failed to identify the pink object racing toward him at an incredible speed. *Oh, a person, an enemy*, he thought after figuring it out, but he had no clue why she was running toward him without a gun.

He was going a hundred and ten miles per hour, and Llenn was running at about twenty-five. That was a relative velocity of a hundred and thirty-five miles per hour.

In the second and a half before they collided, the man came to a conclusion.

If I blow myself up here, I'll only take out the one person. Better to ignore them. I'll zoom past and nail the rest.

Blades of light extended from Llenn's hands. Pale, glowing like ghosts.

The Muramasa F9s Pitohui gave her rose three feet from her clenched hands. With a subtle change in direction, she easily extended the line of light emanating from her left arm toward the neck of the enemy riding straight toward her.

His head came off, armor and all.

"Okay, next!"

Llenn stopped running. The soles of her boots scraped along the concrete, creating a thin trail of smoke. Completing that feat of acrobatics—like a jet landing on an aircraft carrier at sea—she then used all of her agility to make an ultrafast sidestep. Just a little shift—that was all.

When the second rider zipped past, Llenn jumped and gently extended her right arm.

"Hoh!"

Her aim was a little bit off. As the rider came hurtling at her at a hundred and ten miles per hour, her blade caught him in the shoulder.

The lightsword passed through him without any resistance, chopping off a significant portion of his height.

The moment the second one died, the first and now headless rider slammed into a metal pole in the road and tumbled to the ground.

"Huh?"

"Aaah!"

The third and fourth riders saw it happen clearly. The little pink shrimp had rushed forward, swinging photon swords in both hands, hacking up their teammates.

The third rider said rapidly, "I'll dodge her! You blow her up!"

"Got it!"

With the best possible strategy in hand, the third rider tilted to his right, using the entire breadth of the road to avoid Llenn. Even with her agility, she couldn't reach him or rush over to catch him in time.

"Heh-heh!" he cackled, certain of victory, as Llenn shot him a baleful glare as he passed.

"Welcome, little bug. Have you come to fly into the flames?"

Fukaziroh's grenade hit him smack on the mark.

Perhaps if he hadn't been staring at Llenn, he'd have noticed the glaring bullet line. Or if he'd stuck to diligently weaving along the road, he could have avoided the shot.

Even those burly protective layers couldn't withstand a direct hit from a 40 mm grenade, though. The explosion separated his armor and body, and the man was dead before he even had a chance to detonate himself.

"Dammiiiiit!"

From the corner of his vision, the last surviving member of DOOM saw his friend explode. He was faced with a split-second decision.

Should he blow up the little pink one right in front of him like the other guy said?

Or should he plunge into the trailer, hoping to take out as many of them as possible?

He made up his mind. He glared at the tiny pink figure approaching with incredible speed, let go of the handle with his left hand, and reached back to pull the little rope on his backpack.

"You!"

*   *   *

"Jump!" Pitohui shouted, and Llenn obliged.

She launched herself off the surface of the bridge to her right.

Toward the swamp thirty feet below.

"Hyaaaaa!"

The moment her body fell below the bridge, a shock wave hurtled past her, level with the ground and just over her head.

As usual, the audience at the bar had the perfect view of the entire sequence.

The second one had gotten hacked up by Llenn's lightsword, the third took a direct hit from a grenade, and the fourth had detonated himself right beside Llenn.

"Aaaaah! So close!"

But she dived off the side of the bridge barely in time to avoid the force of the blast. She made a tiny splash in the river, and by the time the explosion was turning into a mushroom cloud, she resurfaced.

"Goddammiiiiiiiiiiiit!"

The man in the ten-gallon hat screamed like his soul was leaving his body.

Meanwhile, in the waiting area where the dead had to hang around for ten minutes with nothing to do, the other five members of DOOM welcomed their sixth.

"Awww, you didn't make it, either?"

"Sorry. I thought I had a pretty good chance."

"I guess they're the favorites for a reason… They're tough."

"Yeah, super tough. They were formidable opponents! That was fun!"

"Guess we should root for them now!"

"Yeah! Good luck, little pink shrimp!"

The boys of DOOM wore pleased, irrepressible smiles.

CHAPTER 6

Betrayal and Trust

SECT.6

CHAPTER 6
Betrayal and Trust

"Bwehhh…"

She emerged from the river soaking wet, feet squishing in the muck up to her shins, trudging through grass that rose to chest height.

"You did it, Llenn!" Fukaziroh cheered through the comm into her ear.

"Yep, I did it. Ugh, I'm so tired. Thanks for the backup."

The ends of her favorite cap were floppy from the water, and her bangs stuck to her forehead. The mental exhaustion was written clearly on her face, but at least she was smiling.

Thankfully, in *GGO*, all wet clothes and skin dried very quickly. Before she knew it, the ends of her cap would be perky again.

Llenn checked her watch and saw that it was still only 12:34. From the scan to their charge over the bridge to the explosive showdown, those four minutes had been very eventful.

"Nice one, Llenn! Now, I know you're tired down there, but do you think you could find M wherever he's buried? Come back on the left side of the bridge. *Our* left, I mean."

"Yeah, help me out…," M chimed in over the comm.

"You got it!"

Pitohui continued doling out orders. "Fuka, when you're done reloading, watch out for monsters. If you see one, punch it to death."

"Can do."

"Clare, will you inspect the motorcycles they were using? See if they have gas, if the clutch isn't broken, and if the steering still works. If any of them are usable, stand them up."

"What? I don't know the first thing about motorcycles... What did you call it...? A clutch...?" mumbled Clarence, uncharacteristically nervous.

"Then I'll do it," offered Shirley. "You focus on helping out M. Do you need a rope for that, Pitohui?"

"Yes, yes, thank you!"

As Llenn trudged through the muck in M's direction, listening to her teammates talk, she thought, *Oh, I'm so glad I was able to keep them all alive. I'm glad we're still together.*

DOOM had been a fearsome foe unlike any she'd faced before. Llenn's strategy had been an absolute gamble, one that could easily have ended in her death, but thanks to some excellent backup, they'd all made it through more or less unharmed.

Even the toughest battles had a silver lining: They bred confidence if you emerged victorious.

Here we go! Just you wait, Boss! Just you wait, SHINC! She raised a clenched fist toward the sky and quickened her pace.

"Stop!"

She'd very nearly kicked M in the head.

"Enya Totto! Enya Totto!"

"What is that, Fuka?"

"Dunno. Felt like saying it, that's all."

On top of the bridge, the plan to extract M from the swamp was in progress.

Next to the overturned semitrailer, they were using Shirley's mountain-climbing rope to haul him out, with the other end tied around his shoulders and the guardrail acting as a pulley.

Everyone aside from Llenn and Shirley was doing the pulling. They'd easily towed little Llenn up first, and now she was at the ready with her knife for when the first monster showed up, which would be soon. It was 12:36.

Shirley was checking the bikes. She stood up one that was still rideable. It had belonged to the second man Llenn had sliced up. The handlebars were a bit bent, but not to the point of making it impossible to ride.

Next, Shirley went to the first corpse who'd gotten his head cut off—now back in one piece with a DEAD tag floating over his body—and ripped his backpack off him. Until the bodies disappeared, you could procure any items on their person, so this might prove useful.

"Enya Totto! Enya Totto!"

Pulling M out of the swamp was difficult given that he was firmly stuck and heavy to begin with, but thanks to the absurdly high strength stats of Pitohui and Fukaziroh, he came squelching out. After that, it was just a steady tug to get him up the thirty feet to the bridge.

"I bet it would be really funny if we let go right now."

"Fuka, no."

Enya Totto, Enya Totto. Eventually M reached level with the top of the bridge, and he was able to grab on to the guardrail himself.

"Thanks, everyone."

He pulled himself over at that point. His body and M14 EBR were completely covered in sludge. It spilled and flew off him when he stretched. But this was *GGO*, so it would eventually dry and go back to normal.

Shirley twisted her hands around and around as she rolled up the rope. Pitohui said, "Thanks. You're pretty handy with that rope. You use them a lot?" But Shirley ignored her. Pitohui hadn't used the phrase "in real life," but that was the obvious implication. You couldn't be too careful around her.

Shirley stashed the rope in her inventory, then picked up the R93 Tactical 2 off the ground. She switched out the magazine and ran the bolt back and forth, catching with her bare hand the explosive round that popped out.

At 12:37, Llenn called out, "There it is! Up above!"

About ten feet in the air over the center of the six players, a bundle of glimmering lights was forming. That was a scout monster being generated, indicating they'd been stationary for five minutes. Apparently, if there wasn't soil under their feet to break through, they could appear in the air.

"I'll get it if it comes down," Llenn said, approaching the spot beneath it, her knife-wielding hand poised behind her back, ready to strike.

Three seconds later, what appeared to be a monstrous, nasty-looking koala materialized. The lights vanished as soon as it was complete.

"C'mon, back to the forest...," Llenn murmured, timing her chance to slash it.

"Sorry."

Kablam. Shirley fired her gun.

The ordinary bullet the R93 Tactical 2 fired blasted through the koala's torso and vanished into the sky beyond it, turning the creature back into a bundle of floating lights.

"Huh?" Llenn blinked.

"Hey! What's the big idea?! You're not supposed to shoot 'em!" fumed Fukaziroh.

Shirley spun around, hung her long sniper rifle from the sling over her chest, then rushed toward the motorcycle she'd just propped up, leaping over the seat and pressing the starter button that breathed life into the engine.

"C'mon!"

"Here I am!" replied Clarence. She hauled the backpack of explosives over her shoulders, then hopped onto the tandem seat behind Shirley. She circled her arms around the driver's torso and clapped to give the signal.

Shirley let go of the clutch on the left. The motorcycle squealed into motion, pulling the front wheel off the ground, and they began zooming away into the distance.

"Huh? Hey! What? Why?" Llenn gasped with shock.

"Wah-ha-ha, sorry! So long, suckers!" shouted Clarence as they raced away. The comm clicked as she turned it off.

"What the...?"

"So *this* is where they made their move! Motorcycle and bomb thieves!" Fukaziroh ranted. She pointed the MGL-140s toward the receding bikers but didn't fire. Soon, they were off the bridge and out of sight.

As quiet returned to the bridge, Pitohui suddenly burst into laughter. "Ah-ha-ha-ha-ha-ha-ha! Next time we meet, we'll be enemies! Let's be wary of snipers and explosives, team!"

M's clothes were somehow dry and clean already. He lifted the M14 EBR, checking to see that it was still loaded. "We've got bigger problems to worry about now."

"That's true," said Pitohui, her photon swords back in her hands.

The four of them were now surrounded by a great mass of twinkling lights atop the bridge and in the air overhead. They would begin coalescing into a swarm of monsters momentarily. There was no escape.

"Dammit!"

Llenn pulled her P90 out of storage and yanked the bolt handle.

The audience in the bar watched as the team of four shot and sliced the swarm of monsters descending upon them. They were enjoying the safety of their seats.

"Oh no, you're in trouble now!"

"Good luck with that."

The number of monsters appearing may have increased with time or according to the strength of the squad they were attacking—or perhaps both. The creatures shot up from the ground like grass after rain, and the players had to keep fighting for their lives without a moment to breathe.

The 12:40 scan came and went, but they didn't have a second's peace to stop and look at the results.

*　　　*　　　*

"I'm...so...tired..."

At 12:45, having just shot what seemed to be the last of the creatures with her P90, Llenn let her arms fall to her sides.

Tendrils of white smoke were rising from the muzzle and body of the gun, which had fired and fired and fired over the last several minutes. Many empty magazines lay at her feet.

"Fifteen minutes until we get our ammo refilled... I don't want to do anything...," she grumbled. She crouched and materialized all her remaining ammo magazines to count them.

"I can't believe I only have this many..."

Eight packs left. That was only four hundred rounds. She'd brought twenty-two, meaning she'd used up over half her stock.

Part of the reason for her blowing through her ammo so quickly was that she had to protect Fukaziroh, who was a terrible shot with her own pistol and couldn't use her grenades because the enemy was so close.

"Gosh, sorry about all that. I'll remember this favor you've done me for the rest of my life, or maybe not that long," said Fukaziroh guiltily, stepping out from her hiding spot behind Llenn's tiny back.

She'd been firing her M&P pistol as best she could, but her best was objectively awful. Every now and then, she'd actually hit a monster in the head, to Llenn's delight, only to say, "That's weird... I was aiming for the one next to it..."

"Did anyone see the scan at forty minutes?" Pitohui asked, checking the remaining energy level on her photon swords.

"Nope."

"Nah."

"I couldn't," said Llenn, Fukaziroh, and M in order.

"I was keeping an eye on the bridge, just in case, but I didn't see any enemies approaching. That's a good thing, at least... We'd have been screwed if they'd ganged up on us then," said M. If even he was confessing to potential defeat, then it really had been a bad situation.

"This Squad Jam's a tough one," Llenn admitted.

"So what do we do now?" asked Fukaziroh. "And I'm not asking what you're going to do with the rest of your life."

The first answer came from Pitohui. "I'd like to avoid any serious battle until we get a full ammo refill at one o'clock."

M added, "Agreed. But we can't stay here the whole time. We need to get across the bridge. Let's get ready to move. Llenn in front, then Pito, then me, then Fuka."

Ah yes, I should have known, Llenn thought.

"Load plasma grenades in one of your launchers, Fuka. Destroy them before Llenn makes contact. I don't care if the bridge collapses. We'll escape down the river if it happens. Maybe I'll be too slow and die, but the rest of you can get away."

M's plan put a thought in Llenn's head, so she asked, "W-well... what if Shirley snipes at us as we try to cross the bridge...?"

He replied truthfully, "Let's pray that doesn't happen. There's no way for us to defend against a no-line sniper with explosive bullets."

Daahh! She groaned. She'd have to suck it up.

But even then, she couldn't help but admit, "Man, I don't want to die here..."

"Of course you don't. M, how can a man like you put such delicate young ladies through this hell?"

"But there's no other—"

"Stop. Listen to my idea."

12:49.

The group was moving down the bridge.

They were right next to the guardrail on the leftmost lane. In the lead was M, who wore his backpack over his front and held a plate of his shield in either hand. To his right was Pitohui, who had two shield plates together for defense. To his left, Fukaziroh, with just one.

And behind them, almost completely surrounded as they slowly proceeded, was Llenn.

"Are you sure about this...?"

"Yeah, it's fine! Everyone needs to be a pampered little princess from time to time!" Pitohui said as she stood guard in front of Llenn.

"Well, I appreciate it, but…"

It was true that Llenn wasn't going to take any instant deaths this way. But the rest of them were sitting ducks, and even with the shields, it was a risky strategy.

"If anyone shoots at us, you jump into the river and get away. As we defend, you try to circle around from under the bridge and hopefully get the drop on them. If that's no good, run away on your own and do your best from there."

"G-got it…"

Fukaziroh added, "And if you do get away, tell my girlfriend how much I loved her…"

"Stop making up weird stories."

M ran slowly, so it would still be a while before they crossed the last thousand or so feet of the bridge. Before them was the residential zone along the far bank of the river, the highway bridge, and the airport's control tower.

The sky was clouded over now, swirling with a mixture of crimson and leaden gray. It felt like the wind was picking up, too.

Llenn checked her wristwatch. "Forty seconds to the scan."

"It'll take two minutes to get to the end of the bridge. You watch it come in, Llenn."

"Got it."

"Speaking of the scan," Pitohui said, remembering something, "we might have made it across the bridge if we hadn't stopped to watch it at 12:30, but they'd have caught up to us in the residential area. They had motorcycles, after all."

"That's…true…"

"Then they would have blown up right next to the trailer and possibly killed us all. It was a huge pain, but we're all alive right now, which means that luck and good decisions were on our side. Let's stay optimistic until we're dead, whatever might be coming!"

I feel like it's rare for Pito to talk this way. Is she trying to cheer me up? Llenn wondered. She took her Satellite Scan terminal out of her pocket and switched it on.

The fifth scan started from the east and headed west. It was moving very slowly. Would it be a good thing or a bad thing that they'd be among the first to show up?

"Don't worry about numbers. Focus on the area around us, then look for SHINC and check the results of the battle in the center."

"Roger that."

The scan reached their bridge, and Llenn squinted.

"Nothing! No one within over a mile of us!" she announced, savoring their good luck.

Of course, there could be a leader-mark trap in place, where other members who wouldn't show up as dots on the map were in hiding, but at the very least, there clearly wasn't a swarm of squads waiting for them to finish crossing the bridge.

"One at the airport!" she announced gleefully. That was very likely SHINC's location. Once they were across the bridge, they could charge north toward the airport and maybe get a chance to fight.

She tapped the dot, feeling her heart soar.

"…!"

When she didn't say anything, Fukaziroh asked, "Who is it?"

"Uh…it's MMTM… The one on the runway on the north side of the airport is MMTM… But why…?"

"Dunno. Don't get left behind, Llenn."

She'd stopped walking to think and had to hurry to catch up.

"As for the middle…"

The scan passed the center of the map, revealing a number of gray dots indicating fallen teams around the northern part of the frozen lake. But nearby, though it was difficult to tell against the white color of the lake, there was still a large number of surviving teams.

"Northwest of center, in the middle of the frozen lake, there's, uh, one, two, three, four…*seven* teams all together! That has to be an alliance!" Llenn reported.

"Another one this time. I'll reduce them to plasmic ash," Fuka-ziroh said with a grin.

"Give me the names," said M. Llenn zoomed in the map around the grouping and tapped all the dots, one by one.

"WEEI...V2HG...PORL...," she read. Since she didn't know the official names for the tags, she had to read off the letters individually.

"Don't know these ones."

"RGB...WNGL...SATOH... Aaaaah!" She suddenly let out a scream. That stopped even M.

"What's wrong?" Fukaziroh asked, turning around. Sure enough, Llenn was rooted to the spot.

"Ughhh...," she groaned, device in her hand.

"Hey, is it...?" prompted Fukaziroh.

"Oh no, is it?" repeated Pitohui.

"Oh boy," groaned M, anticipating the answer already.

To the team in the middle of the screen, the rivals with whom she'd sworn a rematch, Llenn shrieked, "Whyyyy?!"

The last of the clustered teams presumably forming an alliance was SHINC.

"Why?!" Llenn wailed to the sky one last time—but she got no answer.

A mighty gust of wind blew across the map of SJ4.

"I'm counting on you," said a tall, handsome man in a tracksuit, white teeth gleaming as he smiled.

"I know. Just leave that little pink one up to us," the gorilla woman said with a grin.

The gust that blew across the frozen lake swung her braided pigtails.

To be continued...

AFTERWORD
Gun Gale Diary: Part 7

Hello, everyone. I'm the author of this book, Keiichi Sigsawa.

It's been a year and three months. Has anything changed in your life?

Sword Art Online Alternative Gun Gale Online (hereafter, "the series") has reached its seventh volume! I'm so happy.

And that means this "Afterword *Gun Gale* Diary," where the author can write whatever he feels like, has also reached its seventh installment.

For the afterwords of the previous six volumes, I discussed how this series came about, my favorite guns, the length of my second toes (which I spoke about quite a bit), my recipe for pork sukiyaki, the tools one needs to change a tire, and even a very simple three-minute method for creating world peace. It's been a wide-ranging segment beloved by all. This time, the topic of choice is "this series is becoming an anime."

Why am I talking about anime? I think you're already aware of this, aren't you?

Yes, as of this writing (June 2018), the televised animated series is airing weekly!

The *Sword Art Online Alternative Gun Gale Online* (hereafter, "Anime *GGO*") started in April and is now in its later stages.

The release date for this book in Japan is Saturday, June 9th, so if you bought this on that date, your TV station or streaming site is going to be airing the show starting at midnight. Have fun! You can also see it in other places, and there will eventually be Blu-rays and DVDs available.

To an anime otaku and writer like me, getting an animated adaptation of one of your works is among the greatest of joys. This one is coming just after last year's adaptation of another series of mine, *Kino's Journey -the Beautiful World- the Animated Series* (hereafter, "Anime *Kino*"), and let me tell you, having consecutive anime adaptations is a whole lot of work.

Among my fellow authors, it's said that there are two good options for how to be involved in their anime. One is "to consider your job done after handing over your original work and patiently wait for the finished product to air in a total hands-off approach." The other is "to become a member of the staff, attending meetings and checking the product, as well as offering new ideas and fine-tuning the end result."

Since Anime *Kino* last year, I've chosen the latter.

So I went to the script meetings, the voice recordings, even the sound effects dubbing sessions, as though I was going to receive a prize for perfect attendance. As of this writing, it's still perfect.

This has led to a huge increase in workload and created an extremely busy time for me.

Of course, this is a good problem to have, but on several occasions, I've thought, *Why did it have to be two series at the same time (airing only three months apart)?!*

For the second half of 2017, I was simultaneously writing Book *Kino*, attending to work for Anime *GGO* (checking scripts and storyboards), and also working on Anime *Kino* (voice-over and effects dubbing, writing exclusive stories for disc releases). It was sheer madness. It felt as chaotic as a festival celebrating Obon and New Year's simultaneously.

There were times when I got an e-mail saying "Check over this by the day after tomorrow," and I panicked because I couldn't tell which thing it was referring to. I can only pray I never actually responded to the wrong person by mistake.

By the time this book comes out, my days of being terrified of e-mail notification sounds are over. At least, I think they're over. I hope they're over. Perhaps I should be preparing for the worst, just in case.

But even so, it's a wonderful thing to have an anime.

I'm reflecting now on what a lucky author this Sigsawa is.

And this time, it's a spin-off. Unlike *Kino*, this isn't a series I created entirely by myself.

From the day Reki Kawahara gave me permission to use the fictional world he birthed and carefully nurtured, I swore to myself, "I can't do anything that will soil the good name of his series. I have to create a story that will be loved by as many people as possible." Even if the descriptions of guns get a little overwhelming.

Now that it's being animated and seen by many more people than before, I feel utterly relieved.

I would be delighted if this little story finds support, huddled in its own gunpowdery corner of the ever-expanding *Sword Art Online* universe.

In Anime *GGO*, you've got Llenn moving and talking and jumping and leaping and shooting like crazy, and it's so adorable. I could practically ask them to change the title to *LCO* (*Llenn's Cute Online*).

I can feel the love for Llenn exuding from her actor, Tomori Kusunoki, and the creative staff. Thank you so much for your work.

Those of you who have seen the anime, or are about to see it, please love our little pink demon. Also, I thought M was cute, too. Especially when he cries.

The staff put a lot of work into the details and depictions of the guns.

There are lots and lots of firearms that make appearances in the series, starting with the main character's partner, P-chan, the pink P90.

Of course, it's got to be animated, so the linework can't be too fine. There are places where we had to alter or simplify the designs. All of those changes were made at meetings where I was present and signed off on them, though, so rest assured that I agreed they were acceptable.

As an example, the stock of Pitohui's favorite gun, the KTR-09, has a very complex shape, so we simplified its look. As a matter of fact, both versions are actual existing options. We just went with the simpler model. There are other changes like this, so if you're a gun freak like me, have fun checking out the details.

But that's enough discussion about the anime.

To talk a little bit about Volume 7 here, after the changeup I threw with the previous volume, I've decided to get back to serious business with the fourth Squad Jam event.

Whoops, was that a spoiler? It was there in the title, you know.

I'll also admit that writing this volume was very difficult! I was balancing it along with all my anime work.

Normally, my books come out in March of any given year, but this time, it ended up in June for a few reasons.

First of all, the bustle of the anime process was going to delay the book by a month.

Then, because of personal business at home, I was unable to put together enough quiet time to concentrate and write, which caused another two months of delay.

I used to think that a professional writer should be able to write no matter what, but the truth is, when you can't do it, you can't do it. I explained the situation to the editorial department, and they understood. I'm very grateful for that. I don't think I'll ever forget this extremely busy and difficult time in my life.

Still, I barely managed to complete the book to get it out while the anime was still airing, so I'm breathing a little sigh of relief right now. Man, that was a close one. Then again, this is just the first part. The story has more to go.

What will happen in the second half?

Will the fourth Squad Jam wrap up safely? What will happen to Llenn—and what will happen to Karen?

Will the second half of this story, containing the answers to those questions, be given a release date by the time this book is on shelves? Or will it still be forthcoming? Everything is shrouded in mystery.

That's all for this time. Let's meet again in the concluding volume of SJ4!

By the way, next time, I intend to fill this segment by writing passionately about "why it's so hard for your right and left hands to engage in a handshake." Look forward to that.

Keiichi Sigsawa

In celebration of the *Gun Gale Online* anime!

Congratulations.

Thank you so much.

When the pink demon zips around,
she's truly a force to be reckoned with!

While drawing the images for this book, I listened to the OP theme "Ryuusei," the ED theme "To See the Future," and the insert song "Pilgrim" on a constant loop.

They're all wonderful songs, and they got me in the mood to draw!

Anime is wonderful!

黒星紅白
Kouhaku Kuroboshi